Praise

POSTER GIRL

"A can't-put-it-down kind of book . . . every moment perfectly crafted to keep the reader turning pages to the gripping end."
—LAURIE BUCHANAN, author of the Sean McPherson series

"A historically accurate, action-packed adventure that makes WWII-era intrigue and sexual and racial discrimination feel contemporary."
—MAREN COOPER, author of *Behind the Lies*

"Casts an observant eye on the misogyny, racism, and classism of the time, allowing the reader to witness that not much has changed."
—MARY CAMARILLO, author of *The Lockhart Women*

"Weaves challenging and timeless social issues into a story about people we grow to care about while maintaining tension and suspense—you won't put this one down."
—ANASTASIA ZEIDEK, author of *Blurred Fates*

"Careful prose, clever plot points, attention to historical detail, and boffo humor bring sunshine and moral perspective to the social challenges of today. An educating and exciting read!"
—JAMES C. SCOTT, archivist for the Sacramento Public Library

"A high-wire, ripped-from-vintage-headlines series-ender."
—GRETCHEN CHERINGTON, author of *Poetic License* and *The Butcher, the Embezzler, and the Fall Guy*

"Mirroring misogyny, racial discrimination, and economic challenges women continue to face today, *Poster Girl* takes readers behind the scenes to experience the toll exacted on women who dared to break molds in the 1940s. A five-star read. Highly recommended."
—ASHLEY E. SWEENEY, author of *Hardland, Answer Creek,* and *Eliza Waite*

Praise for
TOMBOY

"The heroine we need, the heroine we wish we were—determined, tough as hell, utterly loveable. This propulsive novel was a lot of danged fun!"
—ELIZABETH GONZALEZ JAMES, author of *Mona at Sea*

"An intriguing and engaging mystery—readers will hope for more adventures starring the redoubtable hero."
—*KIRKUS REVIEWS*

"Combining the feminist can-do of Phryne Fisher and the snarky commentary of Veronica Mars, Jane Benjamin is a boatload of fun."
—HALLEY SUTTON, author of *The Lady Upstairs*

Praise for
COPY BOY

"Smart, lively, and suspenseful—Raymond Chandler for feminists."
—SHARMA SHIELDS, author of *The Cassandra*

"*Copy Boy* is a rewarding historical novel with a ferocious, fascinating lead."
—*FOREWORD REVIEWS*

"A stellar debut, mesmerizing as the fog lifting over Nob Hill. Highly recommended."
—SHELDON SIEGEL, *New York Times* best-selling author of the Mike Daley/Rosie Fernandez novels

POSTER
GIRL

POSTER GIRL

A Jane Benjamin Novel

SHELLEY BLANTON-STROUD

SHE WRITES PRESS

Copyright © 2023, Shelley Blanton-Stroud

All rights reserved. No part of this publication may be reproduced, distributed, or transmitted in any form or by any means, including photocopying, recording, digital scanning, or other electronic or mechanical methods, without the prior written permission of the publisher, except in the case of brief quotations embodied in critical reviews and certain other noncommercial uses permitted by copyright law. For permission requests, please address She Writes Press.

Published 2023
Printed in the United States of America
Print ISBN: 978-1-64742-593-7
E-ISBN: 978-1-64742-594-4
Library of Congress Control Number: 2023908860

For information, address:
She Writes Press
1569 Solano Ave #546
Berkeley, CA 94707

Interior design by Stacey Aaronson

She Writes Press is a division of SparkPoint Studio, LLC.

All company and/or product names may be trade names, logos, trademarks, and/or registered trademarks and are the property of their respective owners.

This is a work of fiction. Names, characters, places, and incidents either are the product of the author's imagination or are used fictitiously. Any resemblance to actual persons, living or dead, is entirely incidental.

To my mother, Yvonne, and mother-in-law, Joan,
and all the grandmothers in my family, for doing everything
so well, backward and in high heels.

"Nobody's interested in sweetness and light."

— HEDDA HOPPER

"Philosophically, I don't like doing commercials. But it's a matter of dollars and cents."

— HERB CAEN

"When we are no longer able to change a situation, we are challenged to change ourselves."

— VIKTOR FRANKL

———◦———

CHAPTER ONE

DAY SEVEN

Friday, November 13, 1942
Jane Benjamin's Moleskin Notebook

*S*he'd been told her body was a hymn, a flower, a poem. In the end, it was seven gallons of water in a leather pouch. A perfect conductor of electricity.

The powerful current traveled the axis from her fair right hand, gripping the wand with damp gloves, to her left foot, passing through her chest and all her organs on that route.

Stimulated by electricity, the muscles of her fingers contracted so she couldn't let go of the wand, prolonging the duration of contact, increasing the severity of her shock. Her muscles, ligaments, and tendons tore. The tissue of her hand and foot burnt. Her heart muscle was shocked into total disorder of its rhythm. It stopped pumping and her blood stopped circulating.

Later they told me she lost consciousness rapidly, though when I pushed they couldn't say how rapidly. Neither could they say what she thought in those few moments about her heart failing her once again, though it was a very good heart. Maybe because it was a very good heart. Which caused me to question my own.

CHAPTER TWO

———•———

DAY ONE

8 A.M., SATURDAY, NOVEMBER 7, 1942

Yard Two
Lowe Shipyard
Richmond, California

I had a hangover, so everything about the day seemed special built to annoy me. Camera flashbulbs popped like gunfire. Some kind of rah-rah band played, guys in navy uniforms blaring one of those patriotic songs, not the national anthem but equally annoying, lots of horns and drums, guys pounding their sticks like they were aiming to bust my eardrums, or at least my last surviving nerve. Two flags—one the stars and stripes, the other a silhouette of a ship—each as big as my railcar home, whipped and slapped in the wind roaring off San Pablo Bay at Yard Two of Lowe Shipyard. My work-approved uniform, a black velvet jacket over a silk blouse and ladies' slacks, wasn't cutting it in this wind. It seemed like I might blow off in a gust of other people's patriotism.

Thousands of men crowded round, laughing, boisterous in their uniforms, not the military type but that of the shipyard worker—welders, riggers, electricians, plumbers, engineers, and supervisors, their dark jumpsuits, jeans, plaid flannels, heavy boots, and helmets signaling the unique dangers of their jobs. Not soldiers, but doers of risky work even so.

We'd gathered in this makeshift city to launch a liberty ship competition, the shipyard aiming to build one faster than any before it, to send it out to sea in service of the American war effort in under a week. Or, if truth be told, to capture all the headlines possible in seven days, so that shipyard owner Adam Lowe could collect even more wartime business than he already had, which would have been reason enough for me to dislike him. Nobody understood the need for publicity better than me. Almost nobody. But they shouldn't have dressed it up like it was anything other than commerce. That part made me sick. I was only twenty-two but precocious, having ingested cynicism with Momma's milk.

A long black Lincoln rolled up, parking right next to where I stood in a crowd with the rest of the press and propaganda crew. The driver raced around and opened the back door and a woman stepped out, wearing a ridiculous black hat with enormous white flowers, topping the impressive shoulder padding of her bright pink suit. She laughed, her mouth wide open. A frenzy of flash-bulbs popped. Patriotism was one thing, but when mixed with Hollywood? Well, that made a story. *Los Angeles Times* gossip columnist Hedda Hopper's arrival officially made this shipyard contest a big-time event. And it put me on high alert. I wanted to be Hedda Hopper.

Not everything about her, of course. But she had a lot of what I wanted, bylines on papers across the country, a syndicated radio show, pre-movie newsreels of her celebrity interviews, and all the money that came with it. Hedda called her Beverly Hills mansion *the house that fear built*. She could make or ruin people. She worked with Hollywood whispers, hearsay, scuttlebutt, and tittle-tattle. Like I did on a much smaller scale. She was a Hollywood tycoon's enforcer, arbiter of morality. Her version of morality, anyway. She'd recently reported poking around the office of Clark Gable's dentist to confirm he'd had his teeth fixed to pass the army's test, revealing the plan before Gable's studio or anyone else knew. Telling such secrets was half Hedda's brand.

But keeping secrets was the other half. Knowing that so-and-so Hollywood star was homosexual and that his marriage to that adorable makeup artist was a sham, and making it clear to so-and-so that Hedda knew, was worth a gold mine. So-and-so provided her with a constant stream of alternative gossip to avoid his love life being ratted out and his career decimated. Hedda's skilled use of information, whether divulging or concealing it, was ice pick sharp.

I'm not saying that's what I wanted, to ruin or make anybody, or to force my moral opinions on other people, not any of that. And I sure didn't want to be cruel for cruelty's sake. But I really, really wanted money. A mansion of my own would mean something, might finally put the sticky tomato fields and red Sacramento dirt behind me. And gossip was the only well-paying newspaper gig they'd give somebody like me, an Okie, high school dropout, willing to do whatever it took. There was a big gap between what I earned and what Hedda did, and I wanted to jump that gap.

I know it sounds crude. But if you didn't grow up in a tent alongside an irrigation ditch, if you didn't pick tomatoes before and after school as a five-year-old, if you didn't have to fight off men on all sides to survive, then don't scold me about how tacky it is to want money. I had never, ever, had enough, even to eat. I made a regular, if minor, living as a columnist for the *San Francisco Prospect*, with my own private, abandoned railcar to live in, and enough cash for drinks at the bars where I gathered stories. Just enough so that I was painfully aware what I earned hadn't yet made me valid. I wanted proof of accomplishment. I wanted a trophy.

Bustling by on the arm of her guide, Hedda jerked to a stop and looked me down and up, smirking. She reached over and straightened the beret on my head, licked a finger and used it to wipe the side of my mouth, where I may have applied my Jungle Red lipstick in too great a hurry. By twenty-two I probably should have had a better grip on the stick, even after an all-night party. "As if you're always in front of a camera, girly. Part of the job." Then Hedda paraded on.

I had left for the shipyard this morning feeling hung over and cranky, but not ugly and unprofessional. Now Horrible Hedda had fixed me good, making it clear she had the *right* to fix me. I didn't think her columns were better than mine, but her contacts and her status were. So many people had power over me. This was a problem.

"Come on, come on, ne'er-do-wells!" The nattily dressed honcho of the Office of War Information—OWI—the propaganda branch of the war effort, waved over the mob of newsmen, photographers, publicity hounds, and radio folks. "Let's get you briefed before this thing starts." He indicated we should follow him back toward a Quonset hut.

I joined the crowd in a knot at the door to OWI's temporary headquarters, with Hedda up front, her head thrown back, laughing again. I marveled that the outlandish hat stayed right on top where it was supposed to be with her head rolling around like that. She must have had military-grade bobby pins and hair spray. All the tools. All the skills.

Only one other woman was part of the group—the all-around

excellent Sandy Zimmer, underemployed wife of my publisher, Edward Zimmer. She moved through the crowd, shaking reporters' hands, delivering charm that made the driest among them tilt in lustful appreciation. It used to bother me how she used her female attractions, but now I just wished I knew how to do it so well. Sandy definitely steered clear of Hedda, though, as if they'd divided the room. Sandy had made an unwanted appearance in Hedda's column a few years before. They were not friends.

That Hedda attacked Sandy in print was proof of her meanness. Sandy was the kind of person who, right after Pearl Harbor, jumped right up and organized a local USO club, offering wholesome entertainment for the soldier boys spending time in San Francisco. She didn't just do the organizing of facilities but also staffed two shifts a week, on top of her work at the *Prospect*, serving coffee and providing a pretty shoulder for soldiers to lean on. She was too young to be a mother figure, but she made a really good big sister to a whole lot of lonely soldiers.

Really, it seemed like almost everybody had found a way to serve after Pearl Harbor, except for me. Things were much the same for me now that we were at war as before—daily columns serving up semi-scandalous tidbits about the people San Francisco thought important. I didn't feel much zeal coming off my readers these days. I even bored myself when I had to read my stories up next to articles about American boys shipping off to war. It boosted my mood a little just to be part of this temporary effort today, to toot the horn of the guys building the liberty ships that were fighting the Führer. Even if I did see it as one more way for the rich to get richer.

"Thanks for throwing in today, boys," said the OWI guy, who introduced himself as Rupert. "And ladies," he added, nodding first to Hedda and then to Sandy, but not to me. I guess my pants, and maybe my misapplied lipstick, were disqualifying. "Of course you can write whatever you like. So long as you keep to the general plan." He grabbed a sheet of paper from a nearby underling, glanced at its notes, and started rattling off details, which everybody scribbled in their notebooks, ending with his view of the big point: "We're gonna show the Krauts and Japs just what happens when they face off against us. Our ships are going to win this. And we're going to make so many ships so fast that the war'll be over lickety-split."

"Do we have to say *Krauts* and *Japs*?" I hollered. "Goes against our paper's style sheet."

A number of guys laughed, some rolled their eyes, and Sandy smiled, like she expected me to ask that. Then she slipped to the back door, probably to rejoin her husband, Edward, who was glad-handing at the grandstand.

Hedda took it upon herself to answer my question. "What's your name, dear?"

Rupert answered for me. "That's Jane Benjamin, of the *Prospect*."

"Jane Benjamin, of the *Prospect*, what part of the paper do you work in?"

"Gossip," I answered bravely.

"Oh my my. I wasn't aware the *Prospect* had a gossip column. Is there anybody interesting in town to write about?" Dammit. I wished Sandy had been in the room to hear this. "Well then, you understand about interpretation and voice and the power of the columnist to say what she wants. If you want to support this effort, use *Jap* and *Kraut*. Those words go further."

I was plenty familiar with words that go further: *Okie, Arkie, picker, commie, babymaker, twilight lovers, friendly sisters, bitch, dyke*. More too, obviously. I didn't use such words lightly.

Rupert moved things briskly away from the topic. "Mrs. Hopper, what an honor to enjoy the boost your signal provides."

Hedda smiled and tipped her head back, raising her right brow as she inspected the rest of the crowd. Not me, though. She'd already done that evaluation and found me wanting. "I am so pleased to help make sure your contribution to the Allied effort is appreciated. You can count on me to spread the word. And to *use* the words that change things!" She flung one arm in the air— *Ta-da*! The writers took their cue, applauding now for Hedda.

I figured they were acting like fans because of the over-seasoned patriotism we all stewed in, but also, I've noticed that people tend to respect success when they're in the company of it. Every single one of these guys would make fun of Hedda in her absence, but with her right in front of us, there was no doubting the power and influence that poured right off her, from tongue to fingertips. The guys appeared to lap it up, in spite of what they must know about the way she wielded truth and lies. Maybe *because* they understood. That's how it generally works for bullies.

———————◦———————

CHAPTER THREE

DAY ONE

9 A.M., SATURDAY, NOVEMBER 7, 1942

Yard Two
Lowe Shipyard
Richmond, California

Adam Lowe stood on the stage like he was born for elevation. His gold, wavy hair held its shape in the wind. His tailored suit fit his wide shoulders and trim waist just so, in a charcoal wool so formal he looked nearly like a general. He held his hands behind his back and his feet apart, as if balanced on the deck of a ship. I loathed the guy, but he did look good. It wasn't 100 percent clear to me why I detested him so much. For years I'd seen him as an unscrupulous sort, the kind of capitalist who'd tractored my family off our arid Texas land. And I'd seen him treat women badly, in my opinion, controlling them like they were his assets and disposing of them when they'd become liabilities. I'd spent time researching that about him, hoping but failing to find anything solid. Some bones are awful hard to drop.

"Under one year ago," Lowe began in his rolling baritone, "the US Maritime Commission asked us to build liberty ships to aid the Allies in the battle against Axis forces. They expected us to do this building within an extremely tight schedule—two hundred fifty days per ship. Before a year had passed, we were building 'em in sixty days. Then we cut it down to thirty-five days. We're Americans—there's nothing we can't do!"

The bigwigs seated to the side of the stage clapped and beamed. My publisher, Edward, with Sandy by his side, Richmond's mayor, Mattie Chandler, California's governor-elect, Earl Warren, who'd just been swept into office, Hedda, even William Randolph Hearst—maybe the most powerful person at the gathering—applauded and nodded.

I wondered what Lowe did to his people to make them work as fast as that. Then I wondered if it made me un-American to ask such a thing.

"We used our understanding of modern business efficiencies to build 'em by the mile, cut 'em off by the yard!" The audience cheered Lowe's well used line, which was always in the paper. What did that even mean?

"Our ships are built fast, but they're also built well—the very best, according to the officers and crews that sail them. And we're proud of this. Fiercely proud!"

The audience hollered in agreement.

"We've been working hard, and now it's time for a little fun, with a big payoff for our boys fighting on foreign shores, and for all the citizens in the world struggling to get out from under a tyrannical boot!"

I recalled his saying at a dinner once that he didn't care what the government decided to do about going to war. He just aimed to succeed in any economic circumstance war created. This patriotic act today was a ploy to make money, and Lowe played it well.

"In case you're one of the half dozen people here who doesn't know already, our brothers over at Lowe Portland challenged themselves to beat the speed record for shipbuilding, and they went ahead and built the SS *John Sutter* in ten days—ten days! A new world record! Stupendous! Let's hear it for the boys at Lowe Portland!"

The crowd was apparently lukewarm about their brothers at Lowe Portland.

"But hear this. We're going to beat their world record! We're going to show the world why the United States of America can't lose, in this war or any other! We can do this not just because we've mastered the art and science of mass production but because we believe in ourselves, as the world's fastest, world's best shipbuilders!"

He must have read Dale Carnegie's *How to Win Friends and Influence People.*

All of Yard Two exploded in cheers, "World's fastest! World's best!"

Lowe waited for them to exhaust themselves, then held up his arms and yelled, "But that's not all! We're going to build these ships in a way nobody's ever done before."

Manly, expectant roars rose like heat.

"We're going to build our ships with a crew of men *and* ladies, working together." Lowe looked directly at the cameras. "We'd like to introduce you to the first lady welders ever to build a liberty ship."

A small portion of the crowd clapped.

"Mickey Thomas, come on up and introduce these gals."

A beefy guy lumbered up in a suit he seemed to have borrowed from someone two sizes smaller. Three women followed and lined up on stage to his right. He called out names, which I missed. He exuded the enthusiasm of a turnip. Not exactly a cheerleader for the woman welder thing. Might not be so easy for Lowe to coax his shipbuilders' commitment.

I struggled to observe much about the three women at a distance, other than that they wore working clothes, two in jumpsuits, one in heavy pants and a plaid shirt with buttons and patches, two with bandanas around their hair, the third in a helmet. They all wore heavy shoes. One of them had clipped dark, worn gloves to her belt.

Their gumption radiated, riveting me. I rarely saw women who looked so ready to work, as if that was what they were there for, rather than to be decorative. Ever since I'd pretended to be a boy to get my first job at the *Prospect*, I'd learned the difference clothes could make in the way you did your work. It had a lot to do with pockets. Men had them, women didn't, as if men had cash to carry and women didn't, which often enough was true. Where I worked, I was most often the only woman in the room with pockets.

A man in the crowd yelled, "Lift up them pants and show us your ankles!" Others around him laughed. I flushed, angry on behalf of the welder women.

An OWI guy nearby sneered and said, "They're due for a welder welcome on deck."

Another guy said, "Hope they've got a security detail."

The three women walked offstage. The last in the lineup was young and pretty, with bright, light skin, shiny red braids, and a narrow frame. As she stepped away, some men catcalled, one slapping her behind.

She swung around and gave him the one-finger salute, yelling at him and his friends, "That'll be a fiver from each of you or you'll eat my knuckle sandwich."

The crowd laughed.

The woman next in line put her arm around the young one, who rolled her eyes.

"Come on now, men! You're better than that!" Lowe scolded.

He wasn't better than that, I thought.

"These ladies will be our special weapon. Within six months, a deferment will not be an option for men working semiskilled jobs. We'll be sending so many of you to fight, we'll have fewer and fewer to build the ships. Hitler, Mussolini, and Hirohito are depending on that. So we need these ladies, and more. We need our secret weapon! You'll see. We're going to support these ladies in learning to work alongside men because that's how we'll beat our enemies."

He got more applause now.

"And it's not just the beating. We can't let even one man's death be forgotten. We owe it to them. We won't sit and do nothing about it. As our brothers in the marines say, we'll leave no man behind."

Now the crowd applauded raucously as Lowe waved a finish to the speech. The men could swallow the fact of women on their shifts if it was put in that context. They would tolerate it in order to leave no man behind.

Lowe's skills had grown since I'd met him three years before, as had the setting where he showcased them. His booming voice, his physical presence, and the authority of everything he'd created, those flags flying over his head, the massive cranes all around, all the things his money paid for.

The crowd began to move toward the canteen, where a pancake breakfast awaited. The writers raced to the Quonset hut to get their stories down.

I needed to scratch out my story for tomorrow's edition too. I'd emphasize Lowe's glamour but also insinuate something sinister, in that tone I always used about him and guys like him.

But I was dragging my heels, feeling off about the prospect

of writing this usual thing after seeing what I had, after almost feeling the lift of patriotism provoked by those women joining in the effort the best way they could. I had the feeling that writing this piece in the usual way, I'd be diminishing myself somewhat. But that's what I was paid to do. I watched the crowd as it milled away.

Then a whistle blew, then another and several more, and then a deeper horn. A trim fair-skinned Negro woman in conservative suit, her hair pulled back tight, rushed to the stage. She grabbed Lowe's elbow and said something to him that appeared urgent, right in his ear. Adam looked struck. My first reaction was shock. I'd never seen a Negro woman get so familiar with a powerful white man, up so close to his face.

A middle-aged white woman, a little pudgy, dressed like an elementary school principal, pushed away the younger Negro woman and clucked Lowe offstage herself. People all around started hollering, some of them running.

Somebody on stage took the microphone and ordered, "Get to the canteen! Time for the pancake breakfast. Get your pancakes and bacon!"

I was hungry and had a column to write.

But I heard a sizzling, untuned radio kind of static in my head. I waited, everything around me disappearing. The station started to come in, and I heard the familiar voice.

FOLLOW THE WHISTLES.

For crying out loud, Ben, do you always have to do this? I asked silently.

My dead twin brother, Ben, lived in my head, lending his opinions and instincts whether or not I wanted them. He was smart but awful inconvenient. I didn't answer him out loud, obviously. People were right there. I waited for a minute.

He didn't appear to have anything more to say. The normal sounds came back.

I shoved my notebook and pencil in my pocket and trotted after the whistles, as Ben had instructed, rather than toward the pancakes or the typewriters. I ran past cranes and trucks and unfamiliar equipment, pushing my way beyond an ambulance and the first row of gawkers circling a woman's body lying out-stretched on the hard ground of Yard Two.

CHAPTER FOUR

———◦———

DAY ONE

10 A.M., SATURDAY, NOVEMBER 7, 1942

Yard Two
Lowe Shipyard
Richmond, California

She lay at the base of a U-shaped concrete deck, facing the watery bays where five partly built ships lined up, the middle bay empty, like a missing tooth. I heard somebody say her name was Jeannie Lyons.

She lay with her feet toward us, her arm stretching to the water, the sleeves of her dark gray jumpsuit rolled up to the elbows. Her head turned toward her hand, a bandana covering all but a few tendrils of white-blonde hair, safety goggles covering her eyes. Her skin was pale, though I couldn't tell if that was natural or because the life had drained out of her. Heavy boots seemed to anchor her to the pavement. Her gloved right hand clutched a metal wand, attached to a cable. I traced its path, which led to a pole with other cables attached.

"It's this, right here," said a man pointing at a split in the cable.

"She shoulda seen that," said Mickey, the guy from the stage. "Any fella would have seen it."

"Why was it frayed in the first place?" asked a woman crouching next to the body, her face furious. "If you fellas run everything so right, why was it frayed? Tell me that! Sloppy!"

Another man disconnected the cable from the pole.

"It wasn't. I swear it wasn't at the end of shift!" said a man with *Harold* stitched on his coveralls. All the guys around him looked uncomfortable, inching away from the one who may have made the deadly mistake.

Another spoke up on Harold's behalf. "I inspected it before we quit. It wasn't a problem. It had to be her fault."

Harold's face was as red as an August tomato.

Mickey shooed the crowd away. "Go on, we'll take care of this."

I looked around at the dispersing workers.

YOU'RE THE ONLY REPORTER HERE.

I looked at the cable itself. Though the cut was rough, it was definitely a cut, not a wearing away or fraying. "Where are the police?" I asked.

No one answered.

A guy in a medical uniform pulled off the dead woman's right glove to reveal a hand charred like coal, abrupt against the creamy white of her arm. "See the immediate localized rigor mortis here?" he said, illustrating how stiff her arm already was. "The current caused muscular spasm, immediately consuming the adenosine triphosphate, causing the sudden rigor."

I was feeling a little sudden rigor myself.

"We've got extra work to do because of this. This'll put us back," said Mickey.

"Because a dead woman at work probably does slow things down," I muttered.

WHAT A TRAGEDY FOR THIS GUY. EXTRA WORK.

"We gotta get her out of here before the crew starts," Mickey said. "Go on, everybody. We'll check it out and report it. Let the medical guys work."

More people started to scatter, all but the woman crouching next to the body.

Mickey got between me and her. "Get up, Opal. Let him do what he's got to do."

"I'm staying with her, Mickey."

Opal was a lithe, sharp-chinned woman with light brown hair rolled neatly in back of her head, with a bright scarf tied on top. I thought she looked 50 percent pretty, 50 percent pickax.

"I said we need to clear the area," Mickey said.

"I'm not leaving her dead on the ground. I'm waiting with her. I'm sure you understand." Opal's gray eyes said, *Don't push me.*

"Maybe you didn't hear—"

"Let her stay till the victim's gone," I interrupted. "No body left behind, like your boss said?" I kneeled, putting my hand on Opal's sharp shoulder blade.

Mickey steamed at my interruption, an effect I often had on people. "I don't believe that's exactly what Lowe meant." But it didn't look like he was going to fight me on the point.

I stayed next to Opal and the medical technician, as he made notes.

"If she's wearing these work gloves, how'd she get shocked?" I asked.

"They're leather. The voltage she was working with could get through leather. She didn't have rubber lining. And look, they're damp. She was wearing damp gloves. When the boys back in the hospital take off her shoes, her left foot'll be as charred as her hand, I'll bet."

"She was careless," said Opal, ruthless as a preacher's wife.

"You think this was her fault?" I asked Opal.

"That's not what I'm saying."

The technician and I both stared at her, waiting for the explanation.

"It's not her fault the cable was nicked. But it is her fault she wore damp leather gloves with no rubber lining. That's up to each of us. And she should have checked the cable. We're supposed to have learned what to do, in training. It's irresponsible. Incompetent."

Some people are like Opal, able to bypass feelings. I wasn't so practical a thinker. It seemed wrong to talk about the dead woman's carelessness at this very moment, with her right there, her soul maybe still in her body, or hovering above, listening to the judgment.

A truck with LOWE AMBULANCE painted on its side swerved up and expelled three men.

"Clear out, ladies."

The technician began telling them what happened.

Opal and I watched them strap Jeannie to a stretcher and deliver her to the truck. As it raced away, I asked Opal, "Won't the police come?"

"I doubt it. Not the regular police. We're our own little city here. Hospital, safety, childcare, schools, mail. It all stays here, at the shipyard. We handle everything ourselves. Every time there's an accident. They'll take her body to Lowe Field Hospital."

NOBODY LOOKIN' OVER HIS SHOULDER.

"You know a lot about this place, though you mustn't have worked here long. You women welders just started, right?"

"I've been here a few months. Just couldn't weld until now because of the union. Most girls work at Lowe jobs away from the ships. The low-paying jobs. We five got our union cards just in time for the contest, yesterday. Jeannie should have known better. Girls like that make all of us look bad."

My cheeks burned. I don't like bullies. "Why were you staying here with her, then, if you're so critical?"

"Because it's right. Just like it's the right thing for somebody with an opportunity not to waste it for the others."

She was correct about that, though it aggravated me. I'd made hard choices, based on the idea that I was going to do something big, was going to be somebody. I wasn't sure my recent life, either at work or off hours, had justified those earlier choices, or made the road easier for the next girl in my shoes. Opal made me feel guilty, and I didn't like people who did that.

"Anyway," she said. "No man left behind."

That was right too. I had a history of attending to the people left behind, often at Ben's urging. I'm not saying he was some angel on my shoulder. I think he just found it more interesting to ride along with me when I followed the people in trouble than when I followed the rules.

So I'd done the right thing and stayed with Opal and Jeannie. I stood, ready now to get back to work.

AIN'T RIGHT. YOU FEEL IT. DON'T PRETEND YOU DON'T.

Ben was always leaning into my guilt.

MOMMA WAS FIFTEEN years old when she delivered me and Ben alone in a tar paper shack. Scared, crazy from fever, she pulled me out of her, red and kicking, and then pulled Ben out, quiet and blue, a dud, unable to hold a light. She wrapped him in a potato sack, carried him outside, laid him at the side of a barren cotton field, and came back in the shack to nurse me, her big, strong baby.

When Daddy came home that night, he buried Ben in that silty Texas dirt, but Ben's energy never diffused. For seventeen years, he hovered in particles over our heads as we got tractored out of Texas and joined the jalopy migration to California, landing in Sacramento's Rotten Egg Hooverville. He hovered over a muddy irrigation ditch as Daddy and I fought one day when I was seventeen, a crowbar our shared weapon. When Daddy cracked my head with that crowbar, Ben's particles were drawn to me, causing a surge to my filament, making me glow.

That's how I've explained it to the doctors, a time or two, without their fixing anything about the situation. Since that day, Ben has been my near-constant companion. I accept it. Seems fair. Really, it's been kind of a comfort, all these years, to rely on his point of view. But Ben's not in charge of me. I am.

AIN'T RIGHT. YOU FEEL IT. DON'T PRETEND YOU DON'T.

I ignored his commentary, left the scene of Jeannie's tragic accident, and headed to the OWI Quonset to do the job I was paid for.

CHAPTER FIVE

———◦———

DAY ONE

NOON, SATURDAY, NOVEMBER 7, 1942

OWI Quonset
Lowe Shipyard
Richmond, California

The press and PR guys were already hard at work, banging away on the typewriters crammed onto every inch of the metal tables that filled the Quonset hut, sounding like a thousand pinballs plinking against the walls of a giant tin can.

OWI headquarters had no interior walls, just sides and an arched ceiling made of corrugated steel, and two plywood ends with doors and windows cut out. It was cheap and fast to construct, which made sense in a place that so valued efficient assembly, though a problem if you needed privacy. But I'd grown up in a tent, so there was something comforting about the temporary communal shelter, a reminder I didn't need everything perfect to do what I had to do.

I had to type up a bit for tomorrow's *Prospect* promoting the war effort while also dishing a little dirt. I could do it in my sleep. I could play up Lowe's dreamboat persona. That'd be easy. But thinking about it made me sick. I'd rather reveal him as what I suspected he was.

"What have you got?" I asked the guy next to me, who'd paused his typing to smoke, letting ashes sprinkle the desk.

"Straight up. That's my gig. Just the basics, as provided by OWI."

I nodded. One of those guys who never goes much beyond the borders of the press release.

"You?" I asked the one on my other side, with the elbow patches of a professor.

"Where the Lowe liberty ships have gone so far, what battles they've seen."

"Yeah, naturally," I said. People were eager for all the background war stuff, trying to master overwhelmingly detailed content—ships, battles, countries, dates.

"Hey you, *Prospect*," a blowhard across the table bellowed. "I'm doing how they're built—conveyer belt style. Wonder they don't fall apart before they leave the bay. No horning in, right? You'll do what color napkins and cups were provided at the pancake breakfast, right? What flavor syrup?" He was one of those who still used his fraternity voice at fifty.

The guys around me laughed.

"Something like that," I said. I never wrote that kind of thing. But for the moment, truth was, I didn't have an angle. I wanted something relevant, that also popped.

Hedda's awful *har har har* echoed behind me.

"Can't she ever turn the volume down?" muttered the guy from the *Examiner*.

I turned to watch Queen Mean stroll through the middle of our building, her arm on Rupert's, exclaiming, "I'll make some calls. I'll get Johnny Weissmuller here, have him swing off the rig! And maybe Jimmy Stewart can fly in, work the assembly line."

"Everybody loves Jimmy," Rupert answered.

"Boy do they," she leered. "Sometimes too much."

"But what about the ladies?" Rupert asked. "How about getting some starlets in here? That would get attention."

"Yes, starlets are always an attraction. But they're very much in demand right now, for just this sort of thing. Let me think who owes me . . ."

"That would be stupendous. People love to see a pretty lady with their war news."

Jeez. Nothing gets the public going like sex and death. Then I had another thought and grabbed one of the shared telephones on the table and asked the switchboard for the *Prospect*.

"Get me Wally," I said.

A couple minutes later, my buddy was on the line.

"Hey, find me an article about lady welders getting their union cards. I'll wait." Wally sighed, and I could practically hear him making a face.

After a wait, he said, "Here it is. Want me to read?"

"Now, please."

"It's headlined, *Unions Start to Open Doors*. Got a picture of a couple dozen women bunched up, across the desk of some official. Doesn't look pleased."

"Okay, read it."

He recited with the enthusiasm of a fifth grader reading from the dictionary.

Local No. 6 of the Boilermakers, Shipbuilders, Welders, and Helpers of San Francisco felt the woman's touch September 8, when twenty be-slacked lady welders appeared at Headquarters to protest their not being given union clearance for shipyard jobs. The only assurance they received from business manager Ted Raley was that the matter would remain status quo until results of the international's referendum on feminine membership were tabulated. The ladies were silenced but not satisfied.

They'd stormed the office at 155 Tenth Street, demanding the right to work. The feminine influx took Raley by surprise. His first reaction was belligerent. "If these girls attempt a publicity campaign against the union—an organization that seeks to protect women—we'll yank all women workers out of the shipyards and let the government decide who's right."

All sides pointed fingers. Raley declared that adequate restroom facilities had not been installed. A spokeswoman for the protesters retorted: "If we want to walk a couple of extra blocks to a restroom, that's our business and not the union's."

Apparently, direct action worked. The international headquarters of the union today announced from Kansas City that the membership rolls of its six hundred lodges would be opened to women. And now, those ladies can put a new union card in their own pants pockets.

Maybe people did like pretty faces with their war news, but this story also had some actual heft to it. This was a real story.

"Thanks, Wally." I hung up. "Hey, hey, Mr. OWI!"

He scowled. "It's Rupert Graham, weren't you listening?"

"Sorry, Rupert. I need your help."

"What variety of help?"

I tucked my arm in his and pulled him over to the corrugated wall to share what I'd come up with in the small amount of privacy I could arrange.

"Okay, so this contest you've got going is a great big opportunity. Everybody's going to love it—rah rah and all that *Can-Do Adam* stuff in the papers," I began.

"Obviously. And it's for a very good cause . . ." He sounded a bit defensive.

"But there's also this other thing, about the women."

"What about the women?"

"You've got a barrier to getting them into the shipyard. A lot of guys don't like it."

"Lot of ladies don't either. Don't want their shipyard husbands working alongside the girls," he said.

"Or maybe they don't like the idea that *they* should be working here too. Nobody likes to feel guilty."

He clicked his teeth in apparent agreement. "They think it's unnatural. And if you think the girls are a problem, you should hear what they say when we start talking about letting Negroes weld ships with the rest of them."

I didn't expect that barrier would fall any time soon. There were so many battles. That one wasn't mine to fight.

"So you need the women here, because the guys are all gonna be fighting and unless the women start working, your ship production will go down."

"Yeah, yeah, yeah."

"So you need to persuade women this is something they can do, should do. And persuade men that their wives and daughters can and should do it."

"Which is easier said than done, as you may have noticed from the rally crowd." Now Rupert was moping.

"So let's run a campaign right along with the shipbuilding contest. Let's have a contest to find a poster girl, Wendy the Welder, or something." It was brilliant. It would work.

"Winnie the—"

"Wendy, I think. Like you said, people like a pretty girl with their war news."

"I like it," drawled a voice just behind me.

I turned to see Hedda patting the shine off her nose with a handkerchief. She said, "I'll judge the contest at the end of the week. I'll bring in celebrities to consult on the winner."

"Wait," I broke in. "This ain't what I had in mind!" *Ain't.* There it was again, always slipping out when I panicked.

Hedda looked surprised. "*Ain't*, oh charming. I imagine that's your shtick, isn't it? Butter them up like a yokel, trick them into thinking you're some safe nothing? Anyway, it worked for a minute on me. Regardless, I do admire you for coming up with this idea. Fine thinking, yokel."

"No, it's not my shtick." My head was about to spray shrapnel.

"I like it too!" Rupert chimed in.

"This is my story!" I didn't care about compliments. They were stealing *my* story.

Rupert said, "We can run it best internally. We've got photographers, copy guys we like. Please go ahead and write about it from the outside, Jane, incredibly helpful, of course. But we need someone on-site all the time, to get it up and done. And Mrs. Hopper can do the big reveal at the end."

"You're not hearing me. This is mine."

"Don't worry, dear," Hedda said, gripping her jeweled claw on my shoulder. "I'll do it justice. I like your scrappiness. What's your name again?"

"Jane Benjamin," I growled at the woman preparing to make my name irrelevant.

"Give it time, Jane. You're just a baby."

I've never liked being talked down to, even when I *was* a

baby. Especially by somebody working a con. But this wasn't over yet. I could be here on-site full-time. I could make the poster thing catch fire too. Hedda trying to take it made me want it more.

Hedda said, "I'll get girls flocking to work here."

"And their fellas gladly dropping them at the hiring office?" Rupert asked.

"Of course! Who wouldn't want their wife or daughter making good money while helping out the war effort?" Hedda said.

"I'll assume that was rhetorical," Rupert answered.

I seethed at these self-satisfied thieves. People like them always stole from people like me. Reporters ahead of me in the pecking order had taken my stories, slapped their name on them. In a news meeting, I'd pitched good ideas nobody reacted to until a man restated them five minutes after I did. I could not let this stand. Not this time.

I'd jumped plenty of barriers to grab what I had already, fighting for this local gossip column, staying up late every night, learning how to do it. I didn't have natural talent or any training at all. But I had nerve and a willingness to work, and that's what got me here. I was presumptuous.

Maybe that's what moved me about these welder women, their presumption, believing they could do men's work. I was the perfect person for this project because I'd shown that a woman can do a man's work, even when it sometimes had to be done in a skirt. I could do these women justice.

Besides, the story had legs. This week's columns could earn attention coast to coast, and syndication was always on my mind.

But first I had to scoop Hedda. I needed somebody splashy to be the judge. I knew a lot of people who liked to be in the news but only one that fit this scenario: Tommie O'Rourke, tennis champion, nightclub singer, clothing designer, magazine cover girl, and the definition of presumptuous. And she owed me. I'd saved her from an awful headline three years before. If only she wasn't half-crazy or on a bender this week, she'd be perfect.

CHAPTER SIX

DAY ONE

3 P.M., SATURDAY, NOVEMBER 7, 1942

Telegraph Hill
San Francisco, California

When I arrived in San Francisco from the tomato fields outside Sacramento, five years before, I made a study of its neighborhoods, figuring that memorizing what I could about where I lived would make me a real San Franciscan. That didn't work. It's next to impossible to become a real San Franciscan. They won't let just anybody in the club. But it was a useful exercise even so.

I learned that between Telegraph Hill on the east and Russian Hill on the west ran a narrow valley from the edge of the Financial District to North Beach's waterfront. Along its bottom, Columbus Avenue made a diagonal cut, beginning among the shops, cafés, and nightclubs and ending with gasworks, warehouses, and smokestacks. Under a bright blue sky, it looked like a Mediterranean seaside village, tumbling into the sea. Though people said it had been a bohemian neighborhood for struggling painters and poets only a couple decades before, now it offered the shadow of those charms to new renters with bohemian style but banker wallets. Renters like Tommie O'Rourke. Rich people living here gave the whole thing an amusement park feel, like Playland-at-the-Beach or the World's Fair. It was so pretty it seemed artificial.

Tommie's maid, Maria, answered the Greenwich Street door, her hair disheveled under her cap.

"Thank God, Miss Benjamin."

"That bad?"

She made the so-so sign with her hand and sighed.

"I'll go on up."

"Please."

I knew Tommie'd still be in bed after last night's party, which lasted through this morning.

"Hallo!" I hollered as I entered her room—an explosion of pink-and-cream satin and frills, dresses and trophies and black-and-white photos, Tommie always smiling big for the cameras.

"Arrrrrr," Tommie said, her voice croaky from the champagne and cigarettes we'd both overconsumed. "Why are you here at this hour, barbarian? And who'd you go home with?"

That wasn't news worth reporting. I'd left on the arm of a run-of-the-mill *Examiner* sports reporter capable of scratching an evening's itch. A choice not to be repeated, no need to share.

"I need your help," I said.

"So, no kiss and tell? Then go away."

She rolled over and put her head under a pillow.

"Get up, Tommie—I need to talk to you."

Maria came in, balancing a tray with a silver urn of coffee, two white cups, and a creamer.

I nodded and she poured.

"Wake up, Jacob, day's a-breakin' . . ." I sang a few lines of Momma's wake-up song.

"No!!!! I never want to hear from you until at least five p.m." She yelled this from underneath her pink pillow.

I scooted a chair close to her. "Come on, I need to talk to you."

"Good God," she said. "Your head's like a clothes iron."

"This is important."

She propped herself up in bed and glared at me. "I feel sick."

"Bromo Seltzer, please!" I yelled, and Maria arrived as quick as if she'd expected the request.

She mixed it up, and I watched the bubbles rise. "Thanks. Better make that two, please."

And Maria took care of me before she rushed out, closing the door behind her.

"I don't want you. Get out," Tommie said, sipping her medicine through a pout.

"Could you just, for once, be easy?"

"Oh, forgive me, my life's a wreck and you want me to be *easy*. My rent is due, my account is empty, and my last remaining family member has deserted me."

"Frank didn't desert you. He enlisted."

"Same thing. Left me deserted. To handle everything alone."

I honestly did resent the obligation of Tommie since her brother Frank enlisted, and I wouldn't mind some of the benefit of bearing the obligation.

"I need you to judge a contest, for a Wendy the Welder poster girl."

"Winnie the what?" She lit a cigarette, pretending not to be curious.

"Wendy the Welder. These women just got their Boilermakers Union cards allowing them to work on the liberty ships. They're having a huge contest this week—"

"You're talking about Adam's shipyard?" She sounded alert now.

"You know about it?"

"I read the papers." She lit a Lucky Strike from the squashed pack on the nightstand and took a long drag, puffing out a fuzzy ball of smoke that dispersed around an empty bottle of French champagne and two glasses.

"Lowe needs women to work there because all the guys are gonna head off to fight, but everybody's giving him grief, dragging their heels, about getting women their union cards and such. So I'm running a contest." No need to confuse her with the actual status of the contest yet. "I'm writing about the standout women welders this week, and at the end of the week we'll name a poster girl. She'll literally be a poster girl, plastered all over, make working in the war effort look good for a lady. And you'll be the judge of it!"

"I have a busy week. I don't have time."

BUSY DRINKING, CATTING AROUND, AND SLEEPING IT OFF.

"You won't really actually have to judge. I'll judge. We'll pretend you've done it. You'll just be there for the pictures at the end of the week. Just pictures, that's all." I thought *pictures* was the magic word. Tommie loved to be in the newspaper.

"You're exploiting my gorgeousness."

"And the rest of it too."

She sat a little higher in bed and pushed her platinum hair off her forehead. "What day would I have to be available?"

"Wednesday or Thursday? We'll do it the day after they launch the ship."

"We'll see," she said.

"So it's a deal."

"You act like a refrigerator salesman. Okay, but you've got to do something for me."

She fluffed her back pillows up and straightened the blankets on her lap.

Here we go. Why'd everything have to be so complicated? I was already distracted from the poster by thoughts about the dead woman this morning. "What?" I barked.

"Adam wrote me a personal check. I mailed it back when I was in an awful mood. But now I've reconsidered. I want that check. Rent's due. And the other anticipated money hasn't come in. I need his check. That's it. Find the envelope on his desk and get it for me."

"You want me to steal a check off Lowe's desk?"

SHE THINKS YOU'RE HER HENCHMAN.

"Don't act like you've never stolen anything private off somebody's desk before," she reminded me. But that was different. That was three years ago. When I was *really* desperate. "Get me my money."

My irritation turned a corner.

"Your life would be a lot better if you officially broke it off with Lowe. If you keep sleeping with that guy for money, a guy you aren't even attracted to, to say nothing of the complete lack of respect you have for him, it makes you a gold digger. Is that what you want to be?"

"Oh!" She sat up straight, indignation lifting her head two inches higher. "You're hysterical. You're a liar. No, you're *the* liar. You're constantly fibbing and cutting corners to get what you need. I only lie to myself, not to everybody else, like you."

That was true, but that was different.

"Besides, who says I'm not attracted to him? Have you even seen him? He's gorgeous!"

"You were in love with Coach!" I accused.

"Can you hold two things in your head at the same time? Have you ever met even one person who is just one thing and acts that way only for their whole life? Even one person?"

34

"No, but I think you'd be better off if you just slept with people you love or even like rather than this—"

"Blah, blah. The world's mean," she lectured. "If I told the truth about who I am, all the things I am, the world would say, 'Sorry lady, you can't compete in Wimbledon. You can't make any money. You can't talk on our radio show. You can't show your face on a box of Wheaties.'"

She grimaced bitterly, using a miserly voice for the people who judged her, who said no to her. "I don't know about you, but I don't think the truth is worth starving over. I'd rather sleep like a tramp with a well-endowed man, if you know what I mean, and get my rent paid for a year than live like a tramp for even one day." She stubbed out her cigarette as punctuation. "Besides, who are you to give me advice about love or truth? Were you in love with my flyboy brother when you bedded him? Or with whoever the guy was last night? Or the night before?"

She had a point.

"All right, all right," I admitted. "Nagging over. I'll do it. I'll get the check back."

"Okay then. We're not enemies anymore."

Life was long and people need each other. So what if Tommie and I messed each other up a little along the way? My skin wasn't so thin I couldn't get over a few tussles.

"And you'll be the contest judge. You'll show up and be glamorous," I pushed.

"I'll be there. And of course I'll be glamorous. When am I ever not?"

She lit another cigarette, glamorously.

I took a deep breath and ventured the hard part. "Have you heard *anything* from him?"

"Nothing. I can't believe Frank did this to me."

"Stupid idiot, wanting to do something, you know, *meaningful.*"

Tommie pouted. "What could be more meaningful than protecting your little sister?"

"That was a big job. Maybe he wanted something less demanding, like killing Nazis."

———○———

CHAPTER SEVEN

DAY ONE

6:30 P.M., SATURDAY, NOVEMBER 7, 1942

The Prospect Building
Fifth and Mission
San Franciso, California

I steered my 1935 Ford into a lucky spot right in front of the *Prospect*. I didn't have a coin for the guy sleeping next to the front door, but I gave him an OWI donut I'd stashed in my pocket before heading back to the one place I'd ever really considered home.

The newspaper business is addictive, like smoking or drinking. And it's bad for you too, unless you like the idea of becoming progressively cynical while also ironically sentimental about people and places. Running up the *Prospect*'s central staircase always set me buzzing. With every step, I could feel the intoxicating hope of advancement at this place I loved.

That rise wasn't something experienced by all the women in the building, women who were pushed into closets, groped, ridiculed. By pretending to be a boy, Ben, in my early days at the *Prospect*, I wasn't subjected to the humiliating hazing. But I saw plenty of young women run out of that building crying, replacements lined up two days later. It sharpened my ability to smell a rat. I was grateful to have learned these things early.

I'd started on the long copy-boy bench, where six guys sat waiting to jump whenever somebody called, "Boy!" We didn't have names on the bench. We were all *Boy*. It was efficient. But it did stoke my desire to be seen, recognized, known. I wanted to be completely inside the *Prospect*'s machinery, its cogs and chutes, to pass through it with everybody else but to come out special.

Now here I was, a twenty-two-year-old columnist, known as a woman but allowed to wear pants with pockets, as long as I made sure of the lipstick and earrings and other such feminine stuff. I was comfortable and confident at the *Prospect* now, maybe even hitting the ceiling a bit when I stretched these days. So this poster girl thing? It could be just what I needed to get up higher.

I considered how to handle my pitch. Would I go to my managing editor, Mac? Over his head to the publisher, Zimmer? Or over Zimmer's head to his wife, Sandy? The hierarchy here was a minefield. Sandy was smart and capable enough that she should have been running the place. And often she did, in reality. But she did it without an office or a title or official recognition. Also without permission. If it bothered her, she didn't show it. But it bothered me on her behalf.

Though Sandy was my preference, Mac was the first one I approached, as he was my direct, actual boss. He was yelling into the telephone with his office door open. "I said this afternoon! This—af—ter—noon!"

I knocked on his door, doubting the wisdom of the knock.

Mac slammed his telephone down and glared at me. "What now?"

"Hi, Mac."

"I mean it, what now?"

38

"Is this a bad time? Would you rather I—"

"Does it look like this is a bad time?"

It did, truly. Mac's volatile constitution meant his face was capable of turning four different shades of red, as it did now. He pushed back at his yellow buzz cut as if it were drooping in his eyes.

"We've got the printer staff threatening to strike if we don't give them an entirely unreasonable step up in pay . . ."

I wondered whether their pay was already higher than mine at this point or if it was higher than mine would be if I were a man. Probably.

"I'll get out of your way, then." I backed out of the office, whistling. I'd liked Mac from the start. He had a rough background, so he didn't treat mine as a barrier, but he was also a yeller and sometimes I preferred to be the most lively personality in a conversation.

I headed to the corner office of my publisher.

Zimmer sat with his forehead planted on his desk, his right fist thumping the coffee-stained oak. This didn't look promising either.

He raised his head, his face twisted in anguish. A handsome, swarthy man with a square jaw and a booming voice, he'd been awful eligible when Sandy snagged him. But sometimes when things went cattywampus, he screwed up his face like a 180-pound baby. In my book, that made him less appealing. But Sandy had made her choice.

She stood across the desk from Zimmer, placating him with the voice she used whenever he came untethered. "Oh, Edward, it's fine, fine. Just some tweaking of the schedule and we can make it work with a skeleton crew. I'm sure of it. Why don't you let me make that call?"

"No! Did you not hear me before? I'll handle it, Sandy! For Christ's sake. I just have to work it out. Do I have to be cheerful every damn minute? You're making it worse, not better."

I started to back away from the doorway.

Sandy looked up with a wrinkled brow. Then it smoothed and she actually smiled.

I waved at her, tentative, not sure I wanted to interrupt.

She nodded slightly at me, her curly hair bouncing, careful not to alarm the moaning Zimmer with her offensive sunny energy. Didn't she ever tire of talking him down from all the ledges he clung to in a typical work week?

Stable, competent, and cheerful, Sandy was almost always the best bet for getting things done. It ground my gears that she didn't have the verified power to make some decisions, that I had to go through the motions with the guys before I could go to her.

"Edward, I'll be right back, I've just got to . . ." and she was out the door before she'd finished her sentence. His head remained glued to his desk.

I followed her through the hazy newsroom, past cigarette clouds and clacking typewriters and some reporters having a desk drink before going out for a bar drink. We found our way to an empty desk in the corner.

"So what is it today, chickadee?"

It was funny when she called me that. She looked much more like a titmouse than I did, pleasingly curvy and adorable but with sharp enough beak and claws. On Sandy, pretty was also savvy. Her feminine style had gotten her where she was, where she could use her wits, though under the table.

"I've got this great opportunity and I need your help," I said.

"I believe this is the only conversation we ever have. 'Hey, I have this terrific idea, but I've fallen into a pit and I need you to bring a winch.'"

She had a point.

"Sorry. True. Anyway, this time I'm not in a pit, but I still need your help."

I caught her up on the poster girl idea, and how Hedda was poised to steal it by letting OWI guys handle it all week and then swooping in at the end with an actor to name the winner.

"That viper," Sandy said, though I sensed her grudging admiration of Hedda's snaky maneuvers. "How can you get back at her?"

Sandy was a little like me. She did relish a fight, though her punches were less visible than mine, which tended to leave bruises.

"OWI wants control of it, and it is a campaign that might require a lot of shipyard participation. Sooooooo . . . what I'm proposing is—"

"You want to be a hundred percent OWI for the week. Am I right?"

"You're a hundred fifty percent right."

"I'm thinking you'll want to stay there, in the women's residence. OWI doesn't have any women on its publicity staff, so you'll be offering something they can't do themselves, a level of closeness to the lady welders. You should tell them you can be there day and night, interview the lady welders in person, between shifts, so you can choose right. You'll know their real characters, which of them could withstand a little digging. You'll also see who's got the charisma to stand up to the attention."

This was why I loved Sandy. She got things faster than anybody else, often faster than me. I wondered if that was something she learned or if she was born that way.

I said, "I'll also find out who's the best welder. I'll follow them all around on the job."

"I wish I could go with you." Sandy sighed.

I'll bet she wished that. Sandy liked to be in the middle of the action. And not only were things getting negative here, but it sounded like Zimmer didn't want her buzzing around his head. He may not have liked her input, but he definitely needed it.

"Would you please call over to OWI and make it official?"

"Is anybody over there obstructing? Other than Hedda?" Sandy asked.

"This guy, Rupert Graham, in charge of OWI, seems like he wants to live in Hedda's pocket. But there's something else."

"Big surprise."

"One of the women welders died there today. Name of Jeannie Lyons."

"No! That's terrible! I didn't see anything about that coming in. Did you write something? I don't think we sent anybody else over. "

"No. We expected today to be a fluff piece." I shimmered my hands around my face, miming fluff. "They're calling it a workplace accident. No other writers were around to witness it. And they didn't send for police or city ambulance. It's all being handled on-site."

"You're thinking of investigating this apparent accident, no doubt?" she asked, cocking one eyebrow in that all-knowing way.

"Just on the sly."

"I'm guessing you don't want to ruin the poster girl thing because it's a fit with the column."

"Right."

"You sure you don't want me to get someone else to follow up on the dead girl, Jeannie?"

"No, I've got it." I should have said yes. It made sense to say yes. But I didn't want to give it up entirely. After all, I was the only reporter who'd actually seen the result of Jeannie's supposed carelessness.

Sandy gave me a dubious look, then picked up the telephone and directed the switchboard to connect her with OWI and set to work, Sandy style.

"Hello, Mr. Graham? Sandy Zimmer, associate publisher at the *Prospect*. Remember me?"

She wasn't associate publisher, but we didn't actually have one, so she was only borrowing an unused title, though even that could get her into trouble.

"Yes, I'm thrilled at the idea our columnist Jane Benjamin came up with."

Well played. Right to the point—this *was* my idea.

"The *Prospect* wants to support her in doing the best possible job for you and OWI. I understand the shipyard and the government have significant strategic goals involving lady welders. And I just know Jane is the perfect person to handle this for you."

She smiled as if Rupert could see her pink cheeks. He could probably imagine them through the telephone line. She *sounded* pink.

"Mmmmm hmmmmm. Oh, really?" She tapped a pencil on the desk, patient. "Here's what I propose, Rupert. We'll run Jane's columns here as usual, but they'll all be about the welder ladies. She'll belong to you, day and night. She'll stay in the ladies' residence, interview the lady welders, follow them around. We can send a photographer for the posters. She'll be in the best position possible to help you decide who should be Wendy the Welder. We can guarantee you a story every day featuring one of these beautiful patriotic American women."

I wasn't so sure about that. Were they beautiful? Were they patriotic? Or did they just want work that paid their rent? Wasn't that good enough?

"Oh, well of course, Hedda can participate on the big day. But Jane will run it, correct?"

I held my breath.

"Excellent, then."

She hung up, beaming. "Fixed it."

I hugged her. "Sandy, what would I do without you?"

"You'd have been sacked years ago, dummy."

"That is true," I said. "But about all those columns?"

"You're a pro. And about the dead lady . . ."

I said, "Looking into it, definitely looking into it."

"Just don't make too many waves, like you do. One more thing."

"Yes?" Here came the catch.

"You need to completely ace out Hedda."

"What?"

Sandy leaned across the desk meaningfully. "At the end of the week, you need to cut her out. We're not sharing this story with her. Not one little bit."

"But you said—"

"Do you know how hard I hustled to stop her piece on me and Edward after we married? She published it anyway. Made us look like reprobates."

Sandy opened her purse and pulled out her wallet. Folded up in a very small square was a clipping, which she unfolded and set before me on the desk, from a Hedda Hopper column, with one paragraph circled:

How did the former Miss Sandy Abbott find herself in this elevated position as Mrs. Edward

Zimmer? No doubt Mrs. Zimmer was an excellent
secretary to her husband. Or perhaps her ascent
relates to a premarital RMS Queen Mary suite she
shared with the then-eligible publishing
bachelor months before their wedding date. Turns
out, sometimes the best vertical moves are made
horizontally. Hats off to the ambitious Sandy
Zipper!

"Oh yeah," I said, though I hadn't needed the reminder.
How could I forget that column and the tears and hollering
that followed its publication? At the time I'd thought Sandy's
sleeping with Zimmer before marriage had been a predictably
dangerous route to socially acceptable status. My own night-
time behavior didn't seem so dangerous as I wasn't aiming for
100 percent acceptability. Besides, people were somewhat for-
giving of writers. We were a loose lot.

"This is payback, Jane. I am going to best that woman at
every turn. She is not allowed to swoop in and steal this story,
got it?"

I understood the desire for revenge. I've been known to in-
dulge it. Still, it was worrying. Hedda Hopper was a significant
adversary.

"Well, what will Zimmer think?" I asked.

She lifted her chin, confident. "I don't trouble Edward with
every little thing that needs to happen around here."

I'd noticed that and wondered about the arrangement. Is it
normal for a wife to cut her husband out of the loop the way I
regularly saw Sandy do? My own parents always made their
own preferred decisions, which often ran against the other's
best interest. I knew that wasn't a good working model, having
witnessed their knockdown drag-outs. But then I'd never seen
Sandy make a decision that didn't make Zimmer look good,

ultimately, even when he didn't actually choose it for himself.

"Got it," I said, cheered by Sandy's help. "One more thing. Can I cash my paycheck here, now? Just in case of emergency this week."

Another advantage of being buddies with the boss's wife. I left fifteen minutes later with an envelope of cash in my pocket.

CHAPTER EIGHT

DAY ONE

10 P.M., SATURDAY, NOVEMBER 7, 1942

Railcar
Ocean Beach
San Francisco, California

My railcar home sat at the edge of the rough Pacific, situated directly on the sand of San Francisco's Ocean Beach. I paid no rent. It had passed to me through my mother's husband, Jonesie. When Momma made Jonesie trade up to Sea Cliff, he gave the railcar to me, as a fatherly gesture. It was narrow and bare inside, a metal-clad monk's cell clattering in the wind, its cracked windowpanes admitting the ocean's roar. I found those natural sounds purifying after the gossip work I did all day and most nights on the job. I liked my work, but parts of it were kind of dirty.

A few evenings a week, I'd watch my five-year-old sister, Elsie, here, just three minutes down the beach from their roadhouse, Jones-at-the-Beach, where Momma worked nights. I used to take care of Elsie when it was obvious Momma couldn't. But Elsie lived with them full-time now, and she had me part-time, for the fun things, and that was something.

I sat on my bed, feeling the echo of each wave in my body.

I still didn't trust Momma entirely. There was something

ruthlessly ambitious about her, which I understand was an ironic accusation for me to make. But I recalled the ill effects of Momma's decision-making on my childhood. And so I always stayed close, dropping by their house unexpectedly, just to make sure Elsie was okay. I was always ready if things tipped and Elsie needed me.

I felt grateful to have this railcar. I could scarcely imagine a more necessary space for collecting myself, for sorting things out. But now I was working for the chance to maybe have a place of my own. A place that didn't make me beholden to anyone. I saw the difference between what I had, what I valued, and what Hedda had—a mansion built on the success of her career.

I got out my notebook to scribble down the morning's column and call it in.

I scrawled, "The handsome fellas of the Navy Band, decked out in three-piece uniforms, set hearts pounding at the Lowe Richmond Shipyard with their stirring rendition of our national anthem. Horns and drums sent this columnist's imagination to sea, where our fighting boys are doing everything possible to beat the tiny tyrant and his reprehensible Axis henchmen." *Blah blah.*

I continued, "As the American flag whipped majestically above thousands of patriotic shipyard workers, the dreamy industrialist Mr. Adam Lowe himself drove the crowd to tears." I made my own eyes roll.

I explained the shipbuilding contest but then the more exciting news—a poster girl contest. "The new lady welders received wildly supportive cheers from the patriotic fellas, who are glad to fill the shipyard with an outstanding fleet of workers who can make sure the liberty ships keep sailing off to our boys at war, even when the shipbuilding fellas themselves line up to fight. Which pretty face will you see on posters everywhere beginning next week? Watch this space as the story unfurls like Old Glory." *Ugh*, I thought.

Done. That was all I needed, a teaser for the week. I called it in and then readied to pack so I could get some sleep before heading to the shipyard. I was exhausted. But still I was drawn to pull my boxes of notebooks out from under the bed, to read through my research on Adam Lowe. My notes and impressions, every journal, every scrap of paper. Maddeningly, none of it added up to much of significance. Still, this man raised my hackles. I didn't trust him.

Although I knew almost nothing truly incriminating about Lowe, I suspected him of every suspicious thing that happened in his vicinity. I wondered about the dead welder woman, Jeannie. Her name drifted through my head like a ghost, obscuring something else. Why did it sound familiar?

———◦———

CHAPTER NINE

DAY TWO

7 A.M., SUNDAY, NOVEMBER 8, 1942

Team Training Facility
Lowe Town
Richmond, California

Mrs. Pinter had been assigned to deliver me where I needed to go. She moved faster than I expected. She was thick-waisted and shellacked her hair into a brownish-gray cap, facts that together made me expect an easy stroll. Instead she surprised me with a sprint, her heels clopping like a horse over asphalt, dirt, and concrete through Lowe Shipyard, where the construction took place, Lowe Village, with housing and schools, and Lowe Town, where the offices and control center clustered.

I had to learn a little about how to weld in order to write about welding women, and in the welder getup they'd provided, I was walking at a clumsier clip than Mrs. Pinter was. I wore baggy coveralls, a heavy canvas coat, my hair tied back in a scarf, under a heavy headpiece, which were all fine, even good for the wind and wet coming off the bay, but the too-big men's boots made it hard to sprint. Apparently it wasn't easy to find boots like this to fit women's feet, even mine.

Mrs. Pinter hadn't acted real happy to be assigned as my

guide but seemed to have decided that speed was the best way to get through it and back to her desk. She delivered no information on our walk, just waved her arm at each type of building as we whizzed past the fresh new city—canteen, coffee shops, fountains, field hospital, dormitories, childcare centers and schools. Thousands of people rushed to buses, elevated trains, and car lots. The Yard Two day shift had just begun, and the crowds who'd worked the first night shift were rushing home to sleep.

Before the war Richmond had been a lily-white town, but now, with newcomers from across the country streaming in for work, it was at least 10 percent Negro. A nervous energy thrummed through the campus, partly due to the rush of newly arrived citizens into a formerly homogeneous small town.

We arrived at the education building, and Mrs. Pinter slowed to open the door.

"This is where it begins for the women who want to work on the actual ships," she said. She spoke in a very crisp way, like she'd overcome a speech impediment, and she smelled like she'd just baked chocolate chip cookies. "Training takes place twenty-four hours a day. Every crew on-site keeps these hours."

"Even Headquarters?"

"I'm always reachable," she said, straightening the flag brooch on her jacket.

Inside the concrete block building, we stood in a long central hallway where we could see through interior windows to classrooms on both sides of the hall.

"We offer training in every shipyard craft. Each electrician student is taught a specialty. Same with the pipe fitters. We have classes for experienced workers, to advance their trade. And also, of course, your interest, the welding school." She raised her brows, like she was explaining this to a first grader.

Mrs. Pinter clopped to the end of the hall, and I followed. She looked into the last room on the right.

"After six days of training, the students can get to work. We've simplified the welding job, chopped it up into smaller steps, so we can bring people with no previous industrial experience up to speed in just one week's time. When they finish here and pass the test, they head right over to administration, where we get them the union card, even the women now."

"Which was only possible, what, two days ago?"

"That is correct."

"How'd the women get trained in time?"

"They trained here while working at the canteen or housekeeping or other unskilled positions, hoping the boilermakers would relent. Some already knew how to weld, from out in the world. Just didn't have the union card."

"Was that true of Jeannie Lyons too?"

"I don't recall her details."

"Who will be investigating her death? I didn't see any police on Yard Two."

"We complete the full degree of investigatory paperwork for any incident whatsoever."

"Who will look at the paperwork?"

"The authorities." She patted her hair, checking her reflection in the classroom window.

I wasn't the most experienced person around, but even I knew that when somebody said they'd filed a report they often filed it right in the waste basket. Or the alleged reader of the report filed it there. But even when the incident involved a death?

I looked in the classroom. Most of the students were men, only one a woman.

Mrs. Pinter opened the door. "Mr. Farthing, this is Jane

Benjamin, here to learn about girl welders for the newspaper. Introduce her to what she needs to know."

Mr. Farthing smiled and glanced at the female student, not at me, then continued where we'd interrupted him. Mrs. Pinter escaped, *clippity-clop*, her shoes sounding like boots on cobblestones.

Mr. Farthing dropped something in a glass beaker.

"If you put a lump of calcium carbide into water, bubbles of gas will rise." He lit a match. "Ignite it with a flame and it burns. The gas is acetylene. When you mix it with oxygen, it produces the hot blue acetylene flame used in welding."

What an advantage science teachers had over English teachers. Flames were much more interesting than adverbs. His demonstration fascinated me.

"While airplanes require armies of riveters, our liberty ships are welded, not riveted. Here's the equipment you'll use: a cylinder of oxygen, an oxygen regulator, a cylinder of acetylene, an acetylene regulator, lengths of oxygen and acetylene hoses, and a welding torch, mounted on a hand truck. It's all portable. For large-scale welding, the equipment's more elaborate. You can get trained for that next class if you do well enough at this."

I looked around the room, wondering if the woman student would distinguish herself this way.

He held up some goggles. "These goggles or the larger helmet are essential, to protect your eyes from the bright flame and the glare of metal."

Now he wrote on the board as he talked.

"The torch mixes oxygen and acetylene in correct proportions; separate valves regulate the volume of oxygen and the acetylene in lighting. When the acetylene valve is first opened slightly, a lighter strikes a spark . . ."

He went on for quite a while, lots of scientific terms. What seemed interesting moments before now seemed overwhelming and maybe unnecessary for me to know.

"Miss Benjamin, why don't you come up?"

I went cold.

After a second of panic—a test I hadn't studied for, a familiar pattern from childhood—I approached the front of the room, double-checking two layers of gloves on each hand, the first rubber and the second leather, very dry. With a dead woman on deck the morning before, I wasn't taking any chances with damp gloves.

I watched Mr. Farthing check the cables and then the seal on the oxygen tank connections. "Okay," he said, "let's do it together, so you have an idea for your readers."

Standing to my side, he flipped the welding mask down over my face. Everything went dark. Then he put his gloved right hand on my gloved right hand, bringing it and the welding stick I gripped up to the seam.

"Now we'll tap it," he said.

I felt the other students lean in to watch me.

A blue flame leapt and the metal glowed red.

"Closer," he said. And together, his glove and mine, we pressed the wand against the round, glowing pool of molten metal.

The fire leapt from my hand to forge steel. Admittedly, I didn't do that by myself, just moved it under the muscles and bones of Mr. Farthing's hand. But still, I felt the magic of it.

"The bigger the blob, the better the job," he breathed into my ear. Then he squeezed my bottom twice with all the fingers of his left hand.

Everything went dark again except for the flame.

DOES THIS GUY KNOW WHO'S HOLDING THE WAND?

I took a breath and lifted my mask.

I saw nothing but sparks. Then my sight adjusted, and I saw future welders all around me.

"There's your orientation, Miss Benjamin," Mr. Farthing said, patting my behind.

CHAPTER TEN

DAY TWO

10 A.M., SUNDAY, NOVEMBER 8, 1942

Yard Two
Lowe Shipyard
Richmond, California

The repulsive Mr. Farthing suggested I find Mickey Thomas, shipyard supervisor and second unenthusiastic guide. I followed him through the bustling liberty ship construction area, full of finely tuned action with the added spark of the speed contest.

As we moved around the site, voices rose behind me. "She's a new member of the brotherhood. Fuck, fight, or weld pipe!" The men laughed, and Mickey muttered something.

We kept moving.

"Get 'er hot and penetrate," said another guy. "Punch that sheet, every day, all day."

It got so I didn't hear it as we walked, a strategy I'd picked up early on in the newsroom, selective hearing. *Ignore their attitude and get what you want.*

Mickey finally halted and turned, still smirking at the jeers.

"Follow Opal," he said, pointing ahead at the girl I'd met next to Jeannie's dead body. "She's the least useless girl."

Very efficient—Mickey got in a quick insult while passing me off to somebody else.

"You don't really think these women are useless?" I asked.

"I don't have time," Mickey said. "Opal!" he yelled. She approached, mask up. "Let gossip girl follow you. She wants to learn how it's done."

"You said I . . . We're on a timeline!" Opal protested.

"I'm not gonna spare a guy. Besides, this whole mess is about you girls. You brought it, you bear it."

Opal's face reddened. "I'm busy, Mickey."

"Think *we're* not busy?" And he glared at me.

"I won't get in your way," I said to Opal. "I'll just watch."

She stormed off and I followed the storm.

She dropped her mask over her face and picked up her wand. Making the motions the trainer had described, she checked the cable and the seal of the oxygen and acetylene tanks, tapped the wand on the seam, ignited the blue flame, and touched the wand against molten metal. She worked fluidly, so clear in what she was doing that I thought she could be a trainer, standing in front of the room narrating it. When she stopped again and brought up her mask, I asked her how fast would be fast enough in a welding speed competition.

"Mistakes burn time. Better to get it right the first time. Easy, if you've learned the training."

"What do you do if you mess up a weld?"

"You can grind out mistakes. But using a grinder to fix a weld means you're a grinder, not a welder. Who wants to be a grinder?" Her mouth twisted like she was thinking, *Not me.*

Opal cared about being good, but I didn't feature her as a poster girl. Her critical attitude made her objectively pretty face so persnickety nobody would be inspired to leave a Betty Crocker cookbook or a spot in secretarial school to learn to weld ships. I couldn't imagine Opal smiling, for a poster or anything else. A woman could sell almost nothing without a smile.

But she was the only one who'd stayed with Jeannie's body. She had some kind of something the others might not. Opal was a person who didn't just do what was easy.

All manner of workers moved in a gray blur of action around us, along with the roaring fans, whining saws, thundering engines, striking hammers. I took in the noisy assault as Opal worked with such focus.

Then, at the edge of that, I saw the Negro woman I'd watched onstage with Lowe. She stood with her arms crossed in front of her body, lurking in the totally wrong place in her open-toed shoes and navy plaid suit. The look on her face confused me. Was I reading it right? Was it longing?

I touched Opal's arm. "Who's that?"

Opal looked up. "That's Belva. She works in Headquarters. She's a lifetime welder, daughter of a welder, grew up doing it in Oakland with her dad. She can only get the auxiliary boilermaker card. Negroes can't weld our ships. The men in charge won't have it, though she might get closer than others. I guess she's Creole. Some people thought she was white when she got here."

My family never witnessed much fairness by anybody in power, not the farmer nor the banker nor even my own publisher, Zimmer. But I was white and that obviously made it easier, by a long shot.

Belva didn't look like a welder, though of course I had no idea how a welder was supposed to look. She was kind of wispy, and seemed so right in her ladylike clothes, with her smooth, clean face.

"So she's done actual welding jobs, for pay?"

Opal sighed. "Women have been welding for decades. But they've never gotten work in union shops like this because the boilermakers wouldn't let them. Until now, that is."

"She looks too slight for this work."

"Looks can't tell, though I understand you're especially interested in looks, what with your poster contest." That stung, as she intended, especially since the way people looked tended to bore me. I was just working within the existing system, I thought. Opal continued. "All I can say is, I've heard Belva's good. Too bad for her. She'd have been better at this than Jeannie was."

"Seems like you're mad at Jeannie."

"No!" Her face flushed. "Not mad. Just telling the truth. It's a shame what happened to her. It didn't have to. It was stupid."

"You think Belva should have had her spot?"

"She no doubt deserves the chance. Maybe that's why she's got a chip on her shoulder."

"You think they'll change their mind? Let Negroes in? Since they let the white women in?"

"Nothing happens if nobody pushes."

"Don't I know it," I muttered.

"Would you be quiet now and let me work? I'm on a deadline."

So was I, with a contest to arrange, columns to write.

WHAT ABOUT THE DEAD GIRL?

Annoyed by Ben's nudging, I spent my day on Yard Two, watching, taking notes, gathering ideas about welders, like a good girl. I stayed on assignment, except in the back of my mind, which was focused on Jeannie.

CHAPTER ELEVEN

DAY TWO

6 P.M., SUNDAY, NOVEMBER 8, 1942

OWI Quonset
Lowe Town
Richmond, California

I was eating a canteen special Spam and tomato sandwich for supper when the door opened to Belva, hefting a box, which she dropped with a thud on the table where I sat.

"The files you asked for," she said to another guy two chairs down.

"Thanks, Belva," he said.

I peered at her for a few seconds. She stared back.

"You're Jane Benjamin. Have you found your poster girl?" she asked.

"I'm in the middle of it."

"I guess you'd be more likely to find the best girl welder by watching her weld, don't you think? Rather than sitting in here, writing in your notebook?"

SHE KNOWS SOMETHING.

I tucked my notebook and pencil in my pocket and followed her out the door.

"Belva—I'm not sure of your last name."

"Sanders." She walked as fast as Mrs. Pinter, with less horse noise.

"You're a welder too, aren't you?"

"You're a welder if you weld," she spit.

"So what are you then?"

"I'm a clerk. I fetch things."

"You don't act like you think you're some fetch girl."

"Do you act like you think you're a gossip monger?"

I held my tongue about that. "Seems like Mr. Lowe likes you."

"He's all right."

"You're on good terms? He's a good boss?"

Belva stopped walking and sighed. "There are three kinds of jobs I can get. I'm not doing farm work. I lasted one day as a housekeeper. That leaves clerking. That's dicey enough."

"I would think that with clerking, you could rise up—"

"Would you? My first clerking job was for the Civil Service Commission, in the basement of the federal building. I worked in the flagging section. I'd go in, pick up pink and blue cards labeled with the names of people who took the civil service exams. My job was to sort bar-and-flag files. The flag cards were blue. They meant, keep looking for somebody else. The bar flags were pink. They meant, no way will the federal government or defense industry hire him. The ones with barred flags had either been seen in the vicinity of a known communist meeting or were known Negroes."

She let me sit with that for a moment.

"I do okay here because my light skin gives me room. But one time I heard Mrs. Pinter telling Mr. Lowe I was Negro, like he hadn't realized before. I went into his office and said, 'I didn't trick you. I just got transferred here.' He said, 'Don't worry. I don't mind. Everybody here's going to be willing to work with you.'"

She put her hands on her hips and lowered her voice. "Willing to work with me? You know what I thought as I left his office? I thought, *But are they going to be willing to work under* me? I didn't say that bit. I need this job."

So this was the chip on her shoulder Opal referred to. It made sense to me. I'd feel the same way Belva did. I paused before going on, wondering if I could push into another touchy area.

"When I saw you tell Lowe the news about Jeannie, on stage, it looked kind of personal."

"Are you suggesting I overstepped my bounds?" she asked.

"No. How would I know that? I cross lines myself. I wouldn't criticize that in others."

"What kind of lines do you cross, Miss Benjamin?"

I hit a wall with that question.

"Trying to figure whether to tell the truth or a lie?" she pushed.

"No. Just, I've crossed lots of them." There was something about this person that made me want to tell the truth, but my good sense kept that in check. I always had so much to hide just to get my work done. Hide that I was an Okie, that I didn't graduate high school, that my dead brother talked to me in my head. And that I was more ambitious than it was advisable for a woman to be.

She said, "Looks to me like you're happy to work in the box they give you. Hey, I know. I work in a box. I recognize it. I don't like it."

"What do you even—"

"Looks like you're happy to write this dumb gossip poster thing because that's what they'll let you do."

"I'm climbing up the best way I can."

"Maybe you can't imagine another way to climb."

"I don't have time for some guessing game, Belva. I've got work."

"Oh, I know you're very, very busy, Miss Benjamin, doing very important work for the *news*paper."

"Just say it," I said, exhausted. Belva was no pushover.

"There you were, the only *news*person on that deck, sitting there in front of a woman dead because she'd just been welding all by herself. Nobody else was welding because they're all at a rally celebrating the imminent *beginning* to a big welding extravaganza, about to start in another *hour*. So you're there with her dead body. Then not an hour later, you're in that hut with your friends, concocting a really important story about which welder girl is pretty enough to put on a poster."

All of that was true. I shouldn't take offense, but I was easily offended.

"Are you telling me that you do not see Jeannie's death as a welding death?"

"*Jeannie's* death?"

"That's what I said."

"I guess when you're writing gossip, you don't have to find the who, what, when, where, why, and how."

WHOOO BOY! GOTCHA WHERE YOU LIVE!

"If you have something I ought to know, would you please just tell me and stop wasting time?" Now I could hear myself sounding tetchy.

"It would be convenient for me to take all the risks, wouldn't it? Maybe you ought to ask yourself what's worth your taking risks for and what isn't?"

"Are you saying that Jeannie's name isn't Jeannie? And are you saying that Jeannie's death wasn't an accident?"

"I'm saying that you're finally asking the right questions."

She was right. I'd been asking myself who Jeannie was and what really happened to her since I saw her sprawled on the yard. Now I'd finally asked aloud.

We stopped at the threshold of Headquarters, and Belva slammed the door in my face.

CHAPTER TWELVE

DAY TWO

8 P.M., SUNDAY, NOVEMBER 8, 1942

Field Hospital
Lowe Town
Richmond, California

I f I wanted to find out about Jeannie, I'd best start with her body.

The fruity, musty, formaldehyde-and-Betadine smell of the field hospital lobby took me back to hospital smells of my past. It packed enough force that I feared I might pass out.

To the lady manning the front desk, I said, "I need to talk to someone in charge of the woman who died—Jeannie Lyons."

She smirked as if I were a child. "They're busy. They don't have time to talk to you."

I expected this, since it had quickly become clear that everyone at Lowe regarded me as a waste of their time. Reporting could be tedious.

"I'm sure they're busy, but it's important. I'm from the *Prospect*. I need to confirm her identity."

"Maybe you're unfamiliar with medical rules. We can't share information about a patient with you."

"Jeannie's not a patient; she's a dead body."

She snorted. "I suggest you go on over to Headquarters and talk to Mrs. Pinter."

SURE, DO IT. SHE'S AN EASY MARK. THAT'LL WORK SWELL.

I looked around and didn't see an obvious way to get the information I wanted on my own. I needed an actual person who knew about her. That wasn't going to be Mrs. Pinter or this gatekeeping lady.

I stepped outside and waited as several pairs and trios of hospital workers came out for a smoke or to go to the canteen. Finally, a young woman with yellowish fingers came out, her arms wrapped around her middle, a peevish look on her face.

THERE'S OUR GIRL.

"Looks like you could use a cigarette." I shook one out of my pack for her. Dissatisfied smokers were often quite useful.

"Well done, Houdini," she said, accepting my offer.

I pulled a match out of my pocket and reached over to light it for her. "Lady at the front desk is kind of tight with information, you know."

The smoker chuckled knowingly.

"I'm writing about the dead woman for the *Prospect*, and I'm gonna miss my deadline if I can't confirm the accident victim's identity. They're not letting the police in here, and it seems like they'd want her next of kin to be identified."

She blew a smoke ring. "So bureaucratic. Lord."

"I wonder if there's anything you could do to help me. To confirm her name."

She looked at her cigarette, as if wondering what it was worth.

"I could pay you fifty cents," I said.

She took a long drag and then handed the cigarette back to me.

"Let me see it."

"Huh?"

POSTER GIRL

"The fifty cents," she said, patiently.

I pulled it out of my pocket and put the coins in her palm. It was my emergency money.

"Have you got any more?"

From my left pocket I retrieved another twenty-five cents and added it to the rest. Deep pockets helped.

"You want to know her name? Her family?"

"Anything you can find."

She gave me a look like, *Okay, here we go*, but slouched back in the hospital door. I wondered if I'd just wasted seventy-five cents.

I waited outside, distracted, smoking her cigarette until it burnt my finger. I dropped it, wiped off a black smudge, remembering Jeannie's blackened hand. Then I walked a bit away to a bench where I slumped over my notebook, scribbling question upon question to quell my nerves. I didn't care what the front desk lady might think, but Sandy didn't really want me to follow this up and Rupert surely didn't. And if there was a murderer, Lowe definitely didn't want me poking around to prove it. But I *was* a reporter. Sort of. Either my gut or Ben told me this was something significant that could move me out of the range of *sort of* reporter and into something that matters, righting injustice. I thought about Ben egging me on. He died unjustly, and maybe that's why he'd pushed his way into this.

Finally, the smoker came out again. I rose from the bench.

"So this was more interesting than I expected." She sounded a little cheerful now. Snooping had that effect on people, I'd noticed. "The incident file didn't have Jeannie Lyons as the name."

My heart sped.

"Where you're supposed to put the name, they crossed out Jeannie Lyons and put N/A."

"Like—"

"Not available."

"Not available?"

"Looks like they know Jeannie isn't her name, but they don't know what her name is."

This confirmed what Belva hinted, that Jeannie was a fake identity. It set Ben's radio static buzzing in my head about things I ought to do. I tried to ignore him.

"Listen," I said. "What's your name?"

She looked behind her. Nobody there. "Anne."

"Nice to meet you, Anne."

"Mmmhmmm."

"Anne, she's still in there? They haven't already taken her away?"

"Getting picked up any time now."

"Dang it. Where is she?"

Anne smiled, seemingly glad to know there might be trouble. I'd improved her day. "I'll let you in the back door and point the way." She reentered the building through the front doors, and I hustled around to the back, where I found double doors at the right end of a T. I waited a bit before Anne opened the hospital to me.

"Thank you," I whispered. "I better take it from here. Don't want you to lose your job."

She nodded, disappointed, like she agreed but didn't want to go. She walked quietly up the hall and was gone, leaving me with a small pang of melancholy. It had been nice to have a helper for a little while.

I'M STILL HERE.

"Yeah," I whispered. "But I'm not sure you have my best interests in mind."

SO YOU HAVE YOUR OWN BEST INTERESTS IN MIND?

Ben's nagging took up a good portion of most workdays.

I opened the door where Anne had left me. There was Jeannie, on a table in the middle of a very cold room. I'd seen a corpse before, so I knew I'd be all right. Though maybe not 100 percent all right.

I lifted the blanket. In an expanse of creamy skin, Jeannie's charred hand and foot stood out. As the doctor said, the electrical current had passed into her palm, through her body's organs, and out her heel. The directness of that route was shocking. It was obvious *what* had killed her, but not who or why.

I inspected her face, as if I might recognize her now when I hadn't before. That didn't work. I didn't know her. I tried to memorize what I saw. Pale skin, square jaw, wide mouth. Her closed eyes were fringed with dark lashes and, over them, dark shaped brows, though her hair was pale.

Was her hair dyed? Maybe not. Some people had unlikely physical traits. She was beautiful. The kind of woman who doesn't struggle to find love or something close to it, I thought. I recalled Lowe's stricken face when Belva told him on stage what had happened. She had a little scar running through her eyebrow. It made her look so vulnerable.

She was still Jeannie to me until I found out otherwise, still a working woman trying to make her way, like me. I took her charred fingers in mine and lifted them a little, then set them down again on the table. As I turned to go, a glint from below caught my eye. Kneeling, I saw that it came from a fine gold bracelet on the floor below the table. I took it in my hand. Nothing but a tiny chain and a little gold heart. I turned the heart over and got it close enough to read the engraving—*ILI*—before slipping it in my pocket.

CHAPTER THIRTEEN

DAY TWO

10 P.M., SUNDAY, NOVEMBER 8, 1942

Women's Residence
Lowe Village
Richmond, California

After inhaling canteen apples and hard-boiled eggs for dinner, I found the mildewy dormitory room I was assigned to share with the four remaining women welders.

Richmond's population had doubled in the past two years. The shipyard had added 24,000 beds, available at lower than market rate rents. Some workers shared leases, working on opposite shifts, an electrician sleeping in a bed all night, an expediter sleeping in the same bed all day. The place buzzed even in darkest night.

Our room had two bunk bed sets, one single bed, a sink, a mirror, and two dressers. The windows on one side rattled with the wind off the bay, and the sill stayed damp, plump drips sliding down the wall. My roommates all worked day shift, except for Opal, who alternated shifts. She did not share her single bed with a day shifter. The women lounged in the room, slyly inspecting me as I settled in.

Louise Engle talked about her husband named Bob in the

marines and her two grade school kids who lived with Bob's mother in Oakland. Her kids went to the shipyard school and took lunch breaks with Louise before she dropped them at the bus for their grandma to collect at the end of the day.

Louise was gorgeous, with yellow-blonde hair, rounded cheeks, and a pouty mouth. She would have been a candidate for Wendy the Welder, but a darkness under her hazel eyes aged her. Because of Elsie, I knew the kinds of things that keep a mother up at night—her children's nightmares, hurt feelings, bad colds, mean friends. Thinking about Louise raised questions. She might look great on a poster except for those dark circles. They could be painted out.

"Can I help you unpack?" asked Nancy Moore. She looked about my age, with glossy dark hair and a general softness, puffy lips and warm brown eyes.

Before I could answer, "No thanks," she went on.

"The big bathroom's down the hall. Kind of cavernous, but at least we don't have to clean it and our rent's so low!"

"It's great. Just like prison," interrupted a girl with auburn braids.

"Oh, Toots," Nancy said. "Don't be silly. Jane, go ahead and put your things in the second drawer." Her friendly smile converted quickly to a frown. This had to be Jeannie's drawer. "Anyway, we can get all our meals at the canteen down the street. They can even put your food in a bag to take out to a picnic table for a little bit of alone time."

How clever it was to control the workforce by keeping them on-site twenty-four hours a day. But I didn't want to step on Nancy's gratitude.

"Thank you, Nancy." She was after all a welcome counterweight to the gross remarks I'd gotten on deck. I appreciated that. I wondered if there was something almost too pillowy about her to convey what I wanted on my poster. I wanted a pretty woman with a steel spine.

The wisecracking girl with the braids sat on the floor, her back to her bunk, bouncing an old golf ball like a bored ten-year-old boy. I guessed she was straight out of high school. For someone so physically young-looking, skinny and gangly, she had an oddly adult kind of stare.

"And your name is?" I asked.

"Viviana DeNatoli," she said, drawing out each syllable as if speaking to someone who couldn't understand. "But you get to call me Toots." Her pale blue eyes bored into me in an almost-challenge. "Just Toots—Viviana's not the real me."

She was the one who'd yelled at the catcallers at the rally.

She'd look good on a poster but might be too ornery a personality, from a publicity point of view. Who would she cuss out with the world watching? Maybe not role model material.

I looked at a single bed in the corner that no one was sitting on or leaning against.

"That's Opal's," Nancy offered.

It was made up with military precision. I both admired the rigor and felt the urge to jump on the coverlet with my shoes on.

Toots pointed at the bed below Nancy's. "This one's yours—currently unoccupied."

"Auspicious," I said.

I opened my assigned drawer to find Jeannie's things still there. A pair of work pants, a plaid shirt, a nightgown and underwear. When I lifted the shirt, there lay a pale blue leather book with nothing on its soft, worn cover. I felt that shiver that comes with discovering something I'm not supposed to see or know. I hunched over the drawer and opened it to the first page, onto pretty, cursive handwriting. This was Jeannie's diary. I quickly moved her clothes back over it.

"Oh, I can take care of that," Nancy said, standing. "I can ask who to give her things to."

"No, I've got it," I answered, a bit harshly.

Nancy's lips puckered at my rebuke. Louise's eyes rounded. Toots squinted.

I said, "I have to talk to Headquarters and Personnel anyway. They'll know who to pass it along to. But thank you," I said, trying to fix my rudeness.

I dumped my own things onto the bed and pulled my duffel to the drawer, carefully scooping Jeannie's things up into it. I zipped it and set it on top of the dresser. Before anyone could respond, I started asking questions as I put away my own belongings.

"Did all of you go to petition for your cards, like I read in the paper?"

Toots took the lead in her scratchy kid-like voice.

"It was a mix. Opal wasn't part of the petitioning group. That was just me and Jeannie and Nancy. Opal worked in the canteen, doing all the welding training at night in advance, so she was ready when she got the call."

"Why didn't Opal go?"

"She said she's not a complainer," Toots answered.

They all laughed at the apparent irony. Wasn't it Opal who said, "Nothing happens if nobody pushes"?

Toots continued. "She comes from some farm family in Sacramento, no background in welding as far as I've heard. She got good fast. She's the motivated type. Maybe she figured the union cards were going to happen anyway and she didn't need to waste her effort."

Louise spoke up, sounding a little apologetic. "I couldn't get away to go to the union headquarters. My mother-in-law hadn't agreed to take my kids after school yet. I had already enrolled in the training course here at night—that's when she took them— because everybody said I'd earn more money welding. I need more money if I don't want to live with Bob's fire-breathing mom forever." Louise took a long draw on a Chesterfield, then dropped its ashes in a metal ashtray she balanced on her knee. "I have to admit when I first went to welding training, I was a tiny bit ashamed to do such a dirty job. Not exactly office work."

Toots laughed in her scratchy voice. "I was selling cosmetics in a drugstore before I came here. It seemed asinine to sell lipstick during wartime. Then I heard there'd be lots of welding jobs even after the war, so I figured I could go anywhere or do anything with that skill. The union card would be like a passport. I took my training here when everybody said the union might give in. Honestly, it's kind of a relief to get to do dirty work."

"Nancy, how about you?" I asked.

"Oh, Toots and I met working on the housekeeping crew, and she told me I ought to do this. So I did." Nancy looked as if that explained it, but then dug deeper when she saw my expectant expression. "I had my doubts, all through training. On that last day of class, I pulled my hood down, got the stinger out, and started to weld up this bulkhead. So then I took the hood off, and the weld had all run down and looked terrible. I didn't know what to do. I just pulled down my hood and cried. I thought, *I'm too young to do this*. But then I thought, *Well I'm going to try anyway*, so I worked my way up that seam, all the way to the top, and I got it better and better until I knew I could do it!"

Louise smiled support at Nancy, the way you do at a kid.

"I didn't promise anybody I'd be terrifically fast. But I can do the work," Nancy added.

Toots jumped in. "It was girls all over the Bay Area petitioning. Lots of us. We all divided into different shipyards when the union said yes."

With only four left at Lowe Richmond, it was going to be easy to choose. But I asked anyway. "Opal took two of those classes. Is she the best welder among you?"

Toots snorted. "Sure, just ask her."

"She the vain type?" I asked.

"Let's just say, if she were a guy, I know who she'd be."

Now we were getting somewhere. The difference between men and women was always fresh for me.

"Who then?" I prompted.

Toots said, "Some military lemming, who'll march off a cliff. Like infantry or something. She does everything just the way she's been officially taught. And she'll turn in everybody else who doesn't do it that one and only right way, until finally she's the last one standing."

Nancy tried to correct her. "Oh, Toots, that's not—"

"Actually, it's pretty accurate," Louise interrupted Nancy. "Bossy know-it-all, thinks everything's her business."

Toots tossed her ball at Louise, who batted it away so that it rolled back to Toots. Then Toots asked, "Well, what about you, Louise? What would you do in the war if you were a man?"

A smile spread across Louise's face like sun tearing through a fog bank.

"Oh, that's easy. I'd be Bob Hope or Bing Crosby, somebody like that, performing in USO shows for the troops. I'm patriotic, but I'd use my real talents for the war effort." She wiggled her hands on either side of her head, like a vaudevillian.

"Why would that depend on being a guy? Plenty of USO performers are women, aren't they?" I asked, thinking of Judy Garland and Marlene Dietrich and the Andrews Sisters.

"If I were a guy, I wouldn't be married with two kids. I would have been auditioning and getting movie roles in Los Angeles before the war even started, so—"

"Jesus," Toots said. "I'm sorry for your kids."

Louise laughed, not defensive at all, the way some mothers might be. "They do all right."

Then Toots threw the ball to Nancy, who trapped it with two hands, on the nightgown stretched across her lap.

"Go, Nance," said Toots.

"Hmmmmm . . . After Pearl Harbor I would have run down to the firehouse to sign up with all my buddies. We'd do it together. We'd have each other's backs. If we died in battle, I can see our whole town mourning us, putting up a statue."

I thought of all the dead soldiers, how they certainly wouldn't all get a statue.

"Double Jesus," Toots answered.

Nancy tossed the ball back, and we all looked at Toots.

"I'd be the shipyard owner," she said. "Right at the top. I'd control the direction of the war with my executive decisions."

Louise asked, "You'd be a boss? You wouldn't be a soldier?"

"I'd do my part, but I'd make money doing it. I'd get somewhere, instead of having nothing when the war ended. If I were a guy, I'd be running everything. Either that or I'd run off to another country, avoid the war altogether. Maybe get a fishing boat. Maybe in Greece."

The others laughed, like Toots's confusion of purpose was predictable.

She threw the ball at me then, and I caught it one-handed

and shoved it in my pocket, my finger grazing Jeannie's heart charm.

"How about you, Miss Gossip?" Toots asked. "What would you be if you were a guy?"

I thought about telling the truth, that I had a pretty accurate idea what type of guy I'd make. "I'd do exactly what I'm doing right now. Only I'd be further along. Nobody would hold me back. If you're a guy, there's nothing ahead but straight road and a full tank of gas."

I liked the essential truth of my answer, though I was purposely not taking into account the actual experience of my itinerant father, or my dead brother Ben, or Tommie's flyboy brother Frank, or the fact that if I were a guy I'd be facing the upcoming draft. It was hard to hold all the accurate ideas in my head at once, especially when they didn't align with what I already felt.

I sat on my bunk, leaning back against my duffel, stuffed with Jeannie's clothes and diary.

Louise cast her eyes at the duffel sticking out behind me. I couldn't read her smile.

CHAPTER FOURTEEN

———○———

DAY THREE

1:30 A.M., MONDAY, NOVEMBER 9, 1942

Women's Residence
Lowe Village
Richmond, California

When I felt consistent, rhythmic breathing in the bunks around me, I gathered the bundle of clothes I'd tucked under my feet. I inched out of bed, plumping the covers into the shape of a body, and crept to the bathroom down the hall to change clothes, stuffing my nightgown behind a commode. Then I headed for Headquarters.

With the night shift working and the day shift sleeping, there were few wanderers in Lowe Village or Lowe Town and those I passed didn't seem to notice me, camouflaged as I was in welder clothes.

The squat concrete headquarters building sat in darkness, even the front step. The only sound was the deep thump of pile-driving that traveled thick on mist from Yard Two.

I pulled my pick kit out of my pocket.

I lost my keys often enough that I regularly had to break into my railcar apartment. Daddy taught me how. It was his kit I kept with me. We never lived in a home with a lock, so I always wondered what doors he was using it on. I felt no remorse lifting the kit from his belongings one morning years ago. I was saving him from himself.

With my left hand, I inserted the tension wrench into the bottom of the keyhole and applied slight pressure rightward. Then with my right I inserted the pick rake at the top of the hole and scrubbed it back and forth until the lock pins were set. The tumbler turned and I opened the door carefully, to avoid any creaking. Silence. No one responded to my entrance. I closed the door behind me and locked it.

I saw ADAM LOWE painted in gold over a door just ahead. In front of that door, a big metal desk stood sentry, with a placard, MRS. DORIS PINTER, front and center.

A small amount of light slanted through the Venetian blinds, illuminating Mrs. Pinter's desk, neat enough to lick. There was nothing to find there but a gold stand inscribed THANK YOU FOR YOUR SERVICE, with a slot for a letter opener, which was tilted toward me like a knife.

I sat in Mrs. Pinter's chair, swiveling, looking at Lowe's door and the doors to other offices—finance, shipyard operations, construction, site maintenance. I spun back and pulled the knob on each of Mrs. Pinter's drawers, every one of which was locked. I could have tried to pick them open but decided not to take the time. I had to get into Lowe's office and retrieve Tommie's check. I pushed Mrs. Pinter's chair back under the desk.

Lowe's door was also locked. Again I used my kit.

It took a few tries before I got the *ahhhh* feeling of the tumbler turning.

I stepped into Lowe's office and locked the door behind me. It was pitch-black and silent. I felt my way along the wall, bumping my hip into a credenza with a groan.

KLUTZ.

"Shut up," I answered my brother.

I made my way around the credenza to the corner of the room, following the perpendicular wall until I touched heavy, blackout curtains. I lifted just a corner, and the light from the shipyard shone like a spotlight on Lowe's desk near the furthest corner of the room.

I took out my pocket notebook and used it to prop the curtain open a little so I could see.

There were framed photographs on the wall, Lowe on the prow of a ship, Lowe with FDR, Lowe with a crowd of helmeted men at the Hoover Dam he'd helped build. And Lowe in a tuxedo with his fur-coated wife. I got close to that one to inspect her—tall, thin, black-haired. Standing there, her arm hooked in Lowe's, she looked like she smelled something bad. I wondered if she knew about Tommie and the others.

I moved to his desk. Unlike Mrs. Pinter, Lowe kept his messy, with piles of paper. On top were letters without envelopes, annotated in a cramped handwriting, paragraphs circled, exclamation marks and asterisks.

I wanted to read all of it, to take it with me, but knew that was a bad idea. There had to be something in here about the new welders I could use. But first I focused on Tommie's check, turning each sheet over, one at a time, keeping them in the right order, so I could flip them back in place when I found what I'd come for. Then I'd go through the filing cabinets looking for something on the women.

Under the opened mail, I found a pile of letters still in their envelopes, slit at the top, no doubt by Mrs. Pinter's letter opener. She probably read everything on his desk. I rifled through them until I saw Tommie's handwriting on the front of an envelope. I pulled out a handwritten note: "Thanks but no thanks. — T" and a check made out for quite a bit more than Tommie's monthly rent could be. No wonder she'd repented. I tucked the note and the check back into the envelope and put them in my pocket.

I was about to reassemble the desktop mess and turn to the filing cabinets when I saw a yellow legal pad, full of handwriting, some kind of narrative with dates, places, and foreign-sounding names throughout. One name stopped me: "Captain Frank O'Rourke." Tommie's brother.

I went back to the beginning, rereading quickly. On the fourth page, I read that Frank had joined the top-secret Doolittle Raid. Seven months before, on April 18, he'd piloted one of Colonel James Doolittle's sixteen B-25 Mitchell bombers that left the carrier USS *Hornet* to bomb Tokyo, the eighth plane to take off. The Doolittle Raid! All of the crews but Frank's had crashed on the China coast or bailed out. His B-25 had consumed fuel at too high a rate, and so, after attacking his Japanese target successfully, he flew north and landed in a large field, forty miles north of Vladivostok, though Doolittle had told his Raiders not to fly to Russia. He told them to make it to China instead.

This was a lot of baloney. I knew a flimflam operation when I saw one. That raid was all about morale building. It was about propaganda. Oh, we're stronger than the Axis thinks! Oh, we can win this! And Frank was stupid—stupid!—to make himself cannon fodder for a propaganda campaign, when he had his sister to think of. Yeah, I was involved in propaganda, but I wasn't getting myself or anyone else killed for it. That was different.

The raid's morale building had no doubt worked, amping up America's rah-rah spirit, but not all the men came back. And now it looked like that's why Frank was missing, collateral damage in the attempt to convince the folks at home that fighting a war wouldn't hurt us.

Lots of people resisted our joining this war. The America First group argued against wasting American lives on foreign shores. That idea spoke to me. But those Firsters also gave me the heebie-jeebies. It was hard for me to trust anybody who seemed so ardently behind an idea as the Firsters were behind rejecting the war.

Tommie didn't even know Frank had been on this raid. I reread the damning paper, my anger flaring anew at his going down for such an operation.

CALM YOURSELF, GIRL. YOU DON'T KNOW IT ALL.

Okay, so what was Lowe doing with this information? Was he trying to help Tommie? Trying to create more leverage over her than he already had? Could he help get Frank home?

The sound of the front door lock slammed the brakes on my train of thought.

I quickly, silently, righted Lowe's desk. Then I backed into the corner. Crouching in the blackness, I could only see the closest corner of the desktop, lit by the lifted curtain.

A key turned in his lock and Lowe's door opened. Whoever it was would turn on the light and find me balled up in the corner. My heart thumped so loud I was sure the visitor would hear.

They paused, then slowly walked to the window whose curtain was open, just that little bit, propped by my notebook. Was it blank? Had I grabbed the new one? Did it have any of my notes inside?

I was so low to the ground that the desk blocked my view. I couldn't see who was there. But I knew I had to get out before they turned on the light.

I took Toots's golf ball from my pocket and threw it hard at the window, causing whoever it was to holler, which I could barely hear over breaking glass. They dropped the curtain, making it pitch-black again. I ran out of Lowe's office, away from Mrs. Pinter's desk, out the front door, now unlocked. I turned a hard left into the dark and ran away in the unlit alleys between daytime buildings, taking a roundabout route to the dormitory, letting myself in the back door, into our room and my bunk, a dead woman's bed, where I felt Jeannie's diary in the duffel under my ear. But I didn't feel her chain in my pocket. I'd dropped it.

CHAPTER FIFTEEN

DAY THREE

4:30 A.M., MONDAY, NOVEMBER 9, 1942

Women's Residence
Lowe Village
Richmond, California

I lay stiff as a knife on my side, sure the police would come pounding at my door, looking for the person who'd left her notebook behind on Lowe's windowsill. I was pretty sure the moleskin was new, probably blank, but I couldn't recall with certainty there weren't at least a few scrawls that would identify me.

Just who was it, sneaking around Lowe's office in the middle of the night, interrupting my sneaking around his office in the middle of the night? I tortured myself, picturing the worst.

Then I thought again of Jeannie's diary in the duffel under my head.

As quietly as I could, I slipped out of bed again, gripping the duffel and my shoes, and left the dorm. Too late, I realized I'd forgotten a coat. I would have to ignore the cold.

Huddled on a bench in the dark, wet wind blowing in my face, I used the flashlight that came clipped to my work belt to read Jeannie's diary pages, flipping through it quickly, beginning to end, and then restarted with the first entry:

I need him. I need his help. But I feel so much pressure. Even in the personnel office, signing up for my training, I saw how the secretary looked at me, like she knew he'd placed my name on the list. How could she know? She couldn't. So I thought, It's just you and your paranoia. *But after I'd finished the paperwork and was standing to go, she said,* "Training is the leveler. No matter who you are, who you know, you can't get ahead unless you can do the work."

She said it smiling, but was that an attack? Did she think I was there just because of him? Which was obviously true. Really, maybe she said it to everybody, but still . . .

He was fair. He didn't ask anything of me. He understood it had to be over between us, that I couldn't be some other *woman. I told him, if he really loved the person I was, then he couldn't ruin it. He said,* "Yes, I see what you mean." *He said,* "You are a hymn, a flower, a poem. I would never hurt you."

I told myself this risk was right to take.

Jeannie was one of those women who hooked her future to a guy. Probably one guy after another. And Lowe's line—*I would never hurt you*—made my stomach roil at him for lying and at her for being a sucker.

The dark sky began to change to pale purplish gray, and it was time to sneak back into my room and bed. Not long after, at about 6:30, Opal returned from her shift, crawling into her tidy bed, and the day shift started rustling around, preparing for work. I waited until they were down the hall in the bathroom before I jumped up, still in yesterday's welding clothes. I tucked the diary in my interior jacket pocket. After a quick toothbrushing and face rinsing, I decided to follow the first woman out the door. I was going to keep on schedule with the poster project until somebody locked me up for breaking and entering.

CHAPTER SIXTEEN

DAY THREE

6:30 A.M., MONDAY, NOVEMBER 9, 1942

Lowe Village
Richmond, California

Louise was the first to head out in order to pick up her kids at the bus stop and deliver them to Shipyard Elementary before her shift.

I was grateful she walked slower than Mrs. Pinter and Belva. Louise was a saunterer.

"So what exactly is all this poster hubbub about?" she asked.

"They need more women to weld because fewer and fewer men will be around for it—"

"Yes, right, so . . ."

"So I figured we could do what OWI is always doing anyway, making all those posters with messages about the war, you know, bolstering spirit and all. LOOSE LIPS SINK SHIPS, SMACK THE JAPS, JERRY'S WATCHING, all that." I tried to keep the cynicism out of my explanation. This was my idea. I had pitched it. I believed it would work. But still I didn't feel really great about it as an organizing principle.

"So you're doing an advertising campaign."

"More or less."

"What made you decide to use one of us, instead of just an illustration, or a model?"

"Those are options, but I thought the campaign would get better traction with a real woman. She'd have a backstory. She'd be someone people could read up on. There'd be columns, magazine articles, and radio spots. She'd be a hero, in a way."

"Radio spots?"

"Heck, maybe even a song, who knows?"

"Even a song . . . So how much of the backstory is going to be true to life? How much invented?" she asked, interest lighting her face.

"Why do you ask?"

"Natural curiosity."

"It depends what I find out."

"And what you can get away with?"

"I imagine you think you'd be a pretty good candidate."

"Obviously," Louise said. "Look at me. I'm gorgeous, been hearing it every day for just about forever." The way she said it, it seemed like she saw herself at the same time as special, one of a kind, but also somehow disadvantaged. There was something droll about the way she commented on her beauty. Like it was a stupid thing to value.

"You'd look good on a poster. No one has better bone structure, eyebrows, all of it."

"And I'm a ham. I *want* to be on the poster and the radio. I want to be a star. Seems like I'm an easy solution to your problem."

There was something odd about her tone, like her meaning was floating above or below her sentences, not within them.

"Are you trying to tell me something bad about yourself?"

"No, I just anticipate the bad things you might say, about the difference between the way I look and the way I am."

WELL, OKAY, NOW I'M LISTENING.

The gap between two such things *was* usually the interesting part.

"Tell me," I urged.

Louise did look as if she was about to say something but then clamped her lips, her commitment falling short of her intention. "I know what I want. I want this."

I understood. I generally adopted the *I'm perfect for it* outlook myself, though often enough that led me to screech up to roadblocks I might have avoided if I'd thought my route through in advance.

We'd arrived at the stop just as a big white bus with SHIP-YARD ELEMENTARY SCHOOL painted in blue below an American flag pulled up, windows down, kids waving at their mommies and daddies, hollering, "Good morning." These were the kids who lived apart from their working parents.

Louise's eyes tilted at the edges, and her dark brows raised in expectation. The skin under her eyes pinked as a couple of tiny hooligans rushed off the bus and rammed into her knees, hugging her so hard she almost toppled over.

"Granny helped me start my mission project," her freckled boy said. "I chose Mission Soledad. Did you know that means—"

"Oh, I know what *soledad* means, pumpkin," Louise said, laughing. "And how about you, girly?"

"I been coloring between the lines," said the littler one, with bangs expertly curled under.

"Yes, I'll bet you have. I'll bet you made no mistakes. Hey, kiddos, this is Jane. She's gonna walk us to school. Jane, this is Ricky and Susie."

"Hullo, Jane!" yelled Ricky, while Susie hid behind her mother.

We walked the short distance to the school, where crowds of mothers and fathers did the drop-off, lots of running and laughing and crying. It made me think of Elsie, about Momma's maid, Oona, dropping her off in the mornings at Miss Burke's School in Sea Cliff. I felt a pang, not to be the one doing that. I missed Elsie. I usually saw her every afternoon, joining her for an after-school cup of tomato soup and saltine crackers eaten over complaints about a bossy girl or worries over cutting right with scissors.

I stayed and stared, taking in the schoolyard hubbub, until Louise's kids were inside. Then she and I headed to the canteen for coffee and breakfast before the day shift.

"So you want to be the poster girl," I said, returning to the topic at hand.

"Sure I do."

"Why do I hear doubt in that *sure*?"

"Hey, I've lived a life before becoming a mommy welder. Nothing too surprising. It just turns on how fussy you are, whether you'd care."

UH-OH.

"Honestly, it's OWI," I said. "They want a certain kind of image if they're trying to convince men their wives should be associated with this work. I mean—"

"I never believe somebody who says, *Honestly*, so maybe there's my answer," she said, pushing through the canteen doors.

"Wait, what is it? Maybe it's not such a big problem."

Louise turned and crossed her arms.

"I made my bed and I'll lie in it."

I was getting impatient with all this implication.

"What, did you kill somebody?"

"Good question."

THAT'S WHAT I THOUGHT.

My thoughts jumped immediately, though I wondered if I should let my words follow. I did.

"Does it involve Mrs. Burns?"

Louise raised a brow. "Seems like everybody's heard of Mrs. Burns."

"About half the population has."

Louise turned to the canteen counter and said, "I'll take my coffee black."

WHEN I TOLD Momma I was pregnant by Frank, who'd enlisted just a couple months after the single time we slept together, she acted like I had no choice at all: "You're nineteen, you've got the job you want, the fella's gone, doesn't know you're pregnant, doesn't want you."

She didn't mention the biggest thing. I'd been terrible at taking care of my sister. I loved Elsie with every inch of my very tall body, but I'd been an awful temporary mother at nineteen. That was a sore spot with me. I wasn't good mother material, I thought.

Momma said we'd take care of my problem at a place where nobody died and nobody talked, with somebody who knew what they were doing. She wasn't going to take me to one of those untrained hacks set up in hotel rooms rented by the hour, using crochet hooks, coat hangers, and bleach. Lots of women who did it that way, at the hands of such men, wound up on a slab.

Mrs. Inez Burns ran a top-notch, essential service that made her one of the richest women in California. She kept a careful list of her patients. Nearly fifty thousand of them. A very secret list.

So long as nobody died, the police looked the other way.

Her clinic was in an imposing building, with a sign out

front: INEZ BURNS DESIGN. It was two stories, designed to feel pleasant and inviting, with Persian carpets, fancy chairs, oil paintings, and chandeliers. The reception room had her business cards in a copper bowl. The clinic had one operating room, which included surgical devices, a bowl, and a basin. On the ground floor, she maintained two private apartments for patients who needed to recover before leaving through a private door leading to the alley. She'd scheduled me to rest in the private apartment afterward, until I felt ready to go to Momma's house.

In the reception area, a sterling silver tea service was placed on the table before our chairs. I stared at the patterned rug at my feet.

The lady who welcomed me, checked me in, prepared me, wore a clean white nurse's uniform, with a crisp cap. So professional. I didn't know if she was really a nurse.

I looked out the window to the backyard, where I saw the concrete incinerator.

When one of the nurses asked me to follow her up the terrazzo stairs to surgery, she suggested Momma go around the corner to Grant's Pharmacy on Scott and Haight for an ice cream soda while she waited.

The nurse gently arranged me on the hospital table, in a nicer-than-you-might-expect gown.

Mrs. Burns came in, a society lady dressed like a doctor, her coiffed hair smelling of lavender.

She explained what she was doing, every step of the way.

With great confidence, she inserted the speculum, then a dilator, then a catheter, which induced labor. She then inserted a steamed rag to slow the bleeding, calmly narrating everything.

I cramped, yes I cramped, and pressed my fists on my abdomen.

Mrs. Burns removed her gloves, washed her hands, put on new gloves, and came over to squeeze my hand and shoulder.

"You're going to be just fine. Take a couple days to feel better. I'm giving you a dozen quinine pills. Take two every four hours. Then get back to work. Your mother told me you're a girl who's going to do something."

That's what Momma always said. That was the point of me. I was going to do something.

"Thank you, ma'am," I said, truly grateful to Mrs. Burns.

"But Jane, the next time you have sex, I want you to insist he use a condom. If he won't use it, you won't do it. Do you understand?"

"Yes, ma'am." What with all the bourbon we'd consumed, it hadn't occurred to me to do that with Frank that one time we'd had sex. I wondered if it ever occurred to him?

She pulled a small parcel out of a cabinet drawer and handed it to me. "I'm also going to give you a small sponge and a bottle of quinine sulfate. If you're going to do it, make sure that he's wearing the condom and you've inserted the sponge and sulfate. To be extra sure."

I'd never heard these instructions before.

She looked at me with great seriousness. I got the feeling this message was just for me.

"Do these things to make today worthwhile to you. I'll be watching for your name, to see who it is you're about to become."

I expect now that she said this to all her clients. But it felt personal at the time. Very much about me and my future.

They delivered me to the recovery apartment downstairs, where I fell fast asleep under a down comforter, the scent of roses filling my nostrils.

When I heard the yelling and whistles, I knew we were being

raided. The district attorney had finally pulled the trigger that would earn him the headlines he craved.

Cramping, bleeding, I pulled on my regular clothes, which were hanging on the door to my room. I found the back door leading from the apartment to the alley and made my escape, limping to Grant's Pharmacy, where I found Momma sipping cream soda. I sat on a stool next to her and waited until she was done. We caught ourselves a cab and headed back to her home in Sea Cliff, where I slept for two days, before going back to my abandoned railcar apartment and my gossip-writing life, right about the time Mrs. Burns was released from her jail cell to get back to work.

Something about the way these events wrapped up together reinforced my idea that every decision was dangerous, but you get up and get back to work anyway.

But then I had enough experience to know that some people who confront danger don't pop back up and get to work. Some are ruined by disaster, without it being their fault at all. Tragedy triggers a response that is encoded in their bones.

I WONDERED IF Louise had enough experience to understand this too. To understand that some personal history was better left in a sealed box, high on a shelf in the closet.

94

CHAPTER SEVENTEEN

———◦———

DAY THREE

NOON, MONDAY, NOVEMBER 9, 1942

274 Guerrero, Mission District
San Francisco, California

I knocked on the door and soon it swung open, revealing a burly butler who looked more like a bouncer.

"I need to see Mrs. Burns, please."

"I can take a message."

"Tell her it's Jane."

"Jane?"

"This isn't some kind of code. My name is Jane. She knows me. I hardly ever bother her, but I have an important, quick question now."

"What's your last name?"

"Benjamin."

"From the newspaper?" He raised his eyebrow in distaste. An abortionist's butler's insult.

"One moment," he said, closing the door, leaving me on the stoop, an experience that got old.

After a time, the door reopened to the glamorous aging socialite abortionist Inez Burns.

"Jane, Jane, Jane, how are you?" She pulled me into her embrace.

"I'm fine. I'm just . . . checking in." I wrapped my arms around her, which made her grunt.

"Oh, don't worry." She patted my arms. "I've had two ribs removed. Do you like? I don't need stays anymore to get my waist where it needs to be." She wiggled to emphasize her perfected dimensions.

"Couldn't you just have your seams taken out?"

"And give up? What will you think when I tell you I've had my two little toes removed?"

I looked at her extremely pointed, high heel shoes.

"Mrs. Burns! This is getting dangerous, not to mention ridiculous."

"You choose your risks, I'll choose mine. Let's go into the parlor."

I followed her into the darkly paneled room and looked by habit at the fireplace wall.

THAT'S THE SLIDING PANEL, AIN'T IT?

Ben was always wondering about the whispered-about location of hidden compartments where Mrs. Burns stowed her money and medical records.

"So you need an appointment?" she asked directly.

"No, no. I've been doing what you told me."

"The sponge *and* quinine sulfate?"

"And the condoms."

"Good. Then do you want to come to a party?" She glanced at her calendar on the desktop.

"No thank you, this time."

"So what is it you want?" She folded her hands and looked down her nose at me.

"I have questions."

"Only so many questions per person. I believe you've exceeded your budget."

I'd tried to get information out of her months ago, and it hadn't led anywhere productive.

"Listen, we haven't talked for a while. I've been leaving it be, as you said." I tried my best to keep my face sincere—a good little girl who'd followed Mrs. Burns's orders.

"Well done. Exemplary self-control." She smirked.

"But I'm working on something over at Lowe Richmond. It's not about Lowe himself this time. I'm just wondering if there's anything you know about a woman working there, Jeannie Lyons, one of the new women welders mentioned in the paper. Also another one, Louise Engle."

"Sounds like you're still digging around Adam personally."

"I just told you—"

"And I told you the rules. I am not giving you anything. Adam Lowe is a friend. And an excellent contact. And I'm not ruining that with loose talk."

"It's not about Lowe. And you know I'm not some enemy. I'm trying to do good things."

"I've read your column."

"That's mean. And you know there's more to it than that," I begged.

"Are you trying to stir up trouble in Adam's marriage, link him to some woman at work? Your usual kind of hunt?"

"No, not at all. This woman, Jeannie, died at work Saturday. I know you know everybody. Just wondering if you knew her . . ."

"I have nothing to say." Her posture grew even more upright.

"How about Louise Engle?"

"Jane, you say you want to do good things, not make the wrong kind of trouble? Would you like my advice?" She didn't wait for my answer. "Here it is: nobody owes you anything. So be grateful for what they give you anyway."

As if I didn't already know that. It felt like nothing was ever handed to me by anybody. That's why I was so grasping, even if I'd rather not be. I would have loved to be the kind of person the best things flowed to. But that wasn't my life. I had to grab and wrestle for what I wanted. I wasn't in the habit then of inspecting my point of view for its accuracy.

"I'm no fink," she confirmed. "Which you should find comforting."

"I know, Mrs. Burns, I do."

I really did. I didn't want my name to appear on some list of her clients because I didn't want to be arrested or splashed on the front page of my own paper as fodder for scandal, which someone like me might trumpet. I fully saw the irony, but that's the way it was. Also, my abortion had been the right thing to do. I just didn't want to think about it. Thinking about it slowed me down.

Mrs. Burns drummed her nails on the arm of her chair. "You'd expect me never to say anything about our connection, but you'd also like to pump me for information about my connection to other women."

"I'm not doing that," I pleaded.

"You most certainly are."

"I'm not pumping. I just want a simple yes or no answer."

"So if someone, let's say Adam, calls me and says, 'Tell me if Jane Benjamin had cause to accept your services in September 1939. Just yes or no.' You would be all right with my answering?"

"Of course not!"

"And you're a gossip columnist."

I readjusted. "I need to know if I can safely put Louise Engle in the newspaper as a poster girl for the shipyard, at which she would be fantastic and which she would thoroughly enjoy, without also worrying that I would ruin both her life and the liberty ship campaign if it came out that she'd had an abortion."

"You're worried about hurting the liberty ship campaign or about hurting this Miss Engle?"

"Both."

"Then you ought to ask your Miss Engle. I am not telling you anything, one way or the other. My refusing to say anything does not mean anything. I will give you this answer, no matter who you ask me about. I have given this answer when someone else asked me about you."

"What! Who?"

"As I said, I tell no one anything. I can be counted on."

I did appreciate that. But I was alarmed. Someone had been asking about me.

HAS TO BE HEDDA.

CHAPTER EIGHTEEN

DAY THREE

3 P.M., MONDAY, NOVEMBER 9, 1942

Yard Two
Lowe Shipyard
Richmond, California

"Park it right here, Toots!" yelled an electrician, pointing at his zipper.

"Sure thing!" she answered, wiggling her bottom at him and farting like a foghorn.

"What the hell, girl?" He fanned his nose and joined the others in laughing.

"Must be my parking brake. Better get it adjusted," she answered, feigning innocence.

Chomping on a bologna sandwich, Toots joked with the guys nonstop. Even those who'd been gross to me seemed to like Toots, relaxing their aggressiveness. When they said something salty about her looks, she answered with her own crude retort. They laughed with her, unoffended, and she didn't get angry. I was pretty good at ignoring things like sexual jokes and insults, locking them up and getting on with it. But Toots had some kind of personality magic that allowed her to stay loose and easy, even if she was arguing. How did a person get to be like that? Was she so easy by nature or was it an act?

I wondered if she had any resentments at all in this place. I wondered how she actually felt about the men's sex talk.

Though she was pretty, and the men did speak coarsely about her, she was not overtly sexual. She wasn't curvy at all, and moved more like a boy waiting for his turn at bat than a woman waiting to be asked to dance. She had neither that self-consciousness that so many pretty women have that intentionally makes you aware of their looks nor the womanly awareness of men that can make them feel they are being flirted with. No, Toots was lively and interested and practical and direct. She was fun. I was beginning to think she'd make a good poster girl. Except for the fact that she was a sorry worker.

Even I saw her weld seams were messy, that somebody else was going to have to come along after her to clean it up. But it didn't seem to matter as much when Toots did it.

Her skills were passing, so far as I could tell. But a lively conversation would always pull her away from the task at hand. "So where will this ship go?" she'd ask. Or "Why's it got to be welded rather than riveted?" or "What makes our way different than everybody else's way of building them?" The men would jump in to answer: "Most likely the Pacific campaign." "Rivets are too heavy for something that needs to carry a lot of fuel." "We build parts off-site and assemble them here."

She wasn't exactly a role model for women welders. But she was interested and interesting.

Did she have to be a role model? I wondered. Was it enough for a woman to look good and be liked at work? Did she also have to be excellent? Yes, I thought. She had to be everything. I believed in being everything, though I almost never achieved it. But I also liked the way people felt when they were around Toots. Could a poster of her convey that too? I was going to think about it.

"Hey, Toots, can you tell me about Jeannie?" I asked in her smoke break.

"What about her?"

"Your opinion. What she was like. What she was interested in. Her love life. Any of it."

She squinted at me as she inhaled.

"You aren't thinking of making her the poster girl, are you? Like an illustration of her, because she's dead and everybody's sorry and all that?"

I safely stated the obvious. "I don't think a woman dead from welding is the best advertisement for a job as a welder woman."

"Glad you figured that out. So why are you asking?"

"I'm wondering why she was welding right then, during the speeches, when nobody else was welding. When she was supposed to be introduced on stage."

"Neither she or Opal were on stage. Opal's absence was probably stranger than Jeannie's, because Opal's always where she's supposed to be. Then again, she thinks the show-off stuff's stupid. She wants gold stars, not to prance around on stage."

Still, that seemed funny, as Opal looked like the type who wanted credit and getting applause on stage would feel like a whole lot of credit. At least it would for someone like me. Maybe Opal had different standards, though.

"So was Jeannie connected to anybody here? Did she have trouble with anybody?"

"You mean, was she sleeping with Mr. Lowe?"

I LIKE THIS GIRL.

"That's what you mean, right?" she prodded.

"Was she?" I asked.

"People said things. I have no idea if it was true. Don't really care either. What does that have to do with me? Nothing."

I thought again about the look on Lowe's face when Belva told him Jeannie was dead. It had surprised me to see him looking so much like he cared. And if that was true, why would he kill this good-looking girl he was sleeping with, who was also his employee, on the day of this big, public performance? That sounded crazy, even to me, and I hated the guy.

As if she could hear my thoughts, Toots said, "Yeah, I know. Facts confuse things."

"You're smart, Toots."

"Seems like I would have made a better student," she answered.

"You didn't?"

"You don't see me moaning about it like some people do."

"Is there something you really want to do? You said that about running the company—"

"Running what?"

"You said if you were a guy you'd—"

"Oh, that was just talk." She dropped her cigarette and stubbed it out with the toe of her boot.

"Well then, what would you like?" I really wanted to know.

"I want to do everything, see everything, try everything."

"Okay then. Just everything. You'll need money for that, won't you?"

"I'll figure it out. Maybe I'll marry a rich man."

I laughed at that, and she did too. Toots was ridiculous, really. But some ridiculous people are very appealing, I've noticed.

DAY THREE

4 P.M., MONDAY, NOVEMBER 9, 1942

Yard Two
Lowe Shipyard
Richmond, California

"Jesus Christ on a crutch!" Mickey screamed from the mouth of a huge metal pipe before I could utter a single one of my questions.

He wasn't in the right frame of mind to answer them.

"Whose weld is this? Whose?" he yelled.

Workers all around shuffled and cast down their eyes.

"Nancy's," one guy said. "She did that pipe yesterday."

"Nancy!" Mickey yelled.

The circle of onlookers broke and Nancy stepped up, her helmet open. "Sir?"

"You left cracks from the beginning of your weld to the end. Did you not learn proper gas coverage like everybody else trained on-site? Did you not realize we don't do subpar work? We're fast *and* best, Nancy. Do you hear me? We can't afford a bad weld on a ship full of men going to war. If MARCOM heard about such shoddy work . . ."

Nancy's bottom lip quivered as everybody stared. She snorted a sob.

"Now she's crying!" Mickey yelled, even angrier. "We don't have time for crying!"

"I'm sorry, I didn't see any errors yesterday. I'll do better."

"No, you won't! You won't do better! You're off the crew. Get out of here, back to whatever mop or sink or bed you came from."

Nancy froze like a possum.

"Go!"

She walked away, her shoulders raised nearly to her ears.

"Get back to work, everybody. Jim, get in here with the grinder and fix the girl's screw-up."

I had questions for Mickey, but I wouldn't ask them now. Instead I followed Nancy.

"Wait!"

She stood with her mask down.

"I'm sorry," I said. "That was awful."

She pushed up her mask, revealing a very wet face.

"He didn't have to do it like that," I said.

"That's not it."

"I just mean—"

Wrinkles gathered on her forehead. "I don't care how he said it. That's just how he is. But I didn't do that. I didn't make errors. That's not me. I know I'm not the best, but that's because I'm slower than everybody else. But I'm slow because I don't want to make mistakes and ruin it for everybody. I would never . . ." She tried to catch her breath, which came in sip-sized hiccups.

"Well, what do you think he was looking at then?"

"I don't knoooooooooow." Now the racking sobs came. "When I left yesterday, it was right. I know it was. I was upset I didn't finish what I was supposed to, but I wasn't upset that I'd done it wrong."

I didn't know what to say. I felt bad for her. I could tell she was a good person, the kind who probably got stepped on a lot. But I also wondered if she was wrong about this. Maybe she just wasn't good enough to do this work. Maybe she did mess up and didn't realize it. Sometimes good people were also incompetent. I felt guilty for thinking this about Nancy. I liked her.

Then I thought about Jeannie and the possibility in this job for a woman to be asked to do too much, with too little experience, too little training, with too much at stake. Men gunning for them to fail. Even if I wasn't a welder, I was also doing something plenty of men didn't want me to do. I understood it wasn't great to be one of the first, at anything. And here I was, trying to bring more women into this place where mistakes would have such grievous consequences.

Nancy headed away from me back to Lowe Village, and I turned back to the yard, to the roaring of saws and fans and the machinery it took to make steel sail.

To understand what had happened with the flaw, I returned to the dark pipe, lit in the middle with a blue flame, and tapped on a shoulder. The flame went out and a man's mask went up.

"Can you show me the problem with Nancy's weld?"

He walked a little way further and pointed his flashlight at a seam that looked like tire tracks veering off a roadway. "It's like this every little bit. Weird. Maybe she gets tired or something after a certain amount of time and her arm gives out, maybe? It's like this the whole route of the pipe. A good amount of weld is fine and then this breakup."

"Have you ever seen work like this before?"

"Actually, never. It's like a particular welder's pattern."

"The way a person using Morse code has a kind of accent?"

"Yeah, I've heard of that. Except I haven't seen this particular pattern anywhere else on the shipyard. It's like she used it only here, only this time. Then again, she only started work two days ago."

Maybe it wasn't a weld pattern but a sabotage pattern.

CHAPTER TWENTY

DAY THREE

5 P.M., MONDAY, NOVEMBER 9, 1942

Headquarters
Lowe Shipyard
Richmond, California

"Mrs. Pinter, I need some background information about
the lady welders for my article."

"Well then, you'd best go interview them." Her cheeks
glowed pink and satisfied.

"I will do that. I also need the basics. Hometowns, family,
age, all that."

"Sounds like you've got work to do then, sweetie."

She turned her back to me and started typing.

I looked over her shoulder at the wall of filing cabinets. If I
could get in there, I could look up anybody, not just Jeannie.

Mrs. Pinter looked up again and shared that awful double set
of dimples. "Will there be anything else, Miss Benjamin? I've got
such a pile. You know Mr. Lowe's got high ideals."

I remembered what Mrs. Burns said: *Nobody owes you anything.*

"Mrs. Pinter, you always smell so good, like chocolate chip
cookies."

She laughed. "It's vanilla. I put it behind my ears. I find it calms people."

It wasn't calming me, but it did make me ravenous. And why did she need to calm people? "Are you sure you don't have time?"

"No time at all," she answered.

Her hands on the typewriter keys were plump but not pampered. No nail polish. I examined her suit and noticed that the fabric looked fresh and thick, no fraying or shine to suggest it was something old she kept over time, the way most women did. It was hard to judge, but I thought her clothes looked expensive, and I wondered if she was married to someone with a better income than hers. But no ring. Maybe she put everything she had into good suits.

"I'll come back later with questions after I finish with the women," I said, and left.

I was partly disappointed—no information on Jeannie, or whoever ILI was—and partly relieved. Nobody had rushed up to throw a net over my head for breaking and entering.

I had to find answers elsewhere. I strolled slowly from Mrs. Pinter's office. Once out of her sight, I rushed to the dorm and opened Nancy's drawer, above mine. Her clothes were still there.

I wandered through the dormitory, looking for someone to ask if they'd seen her. A woman on the housekeeping staff said, "She's mopping downstairs."

They'd sent Nancy back to her old job.

I rushed down the staircase and up and down the hall, looking left and right into open doors of dormitory rooms, and finally found her in the bathroom, kneeling with a scrub brush, cleaning the grout between tiny black-and-white octagon tiles on the bathroom floor.

"So you got reassigned?" I knew this was heartbreaking for

her, humiliating. "Are you going to stay, under the circumstances?"

"Not in the position to quit." Nancy sniffled. People didn't walk away from a job just because they'd been humiliated in it. I knew that feeling of being stuck in circumstances you didn't cause.

"Nancy, I'm so sorry about this. It's not fair. But I need to ask you some questions."

She stood up and took hold of her mop, leaning on it like it was a cane.

I said, "I know you're a good listener, and you care about people."

She exhaled slowly, like she was venting steam.

"Did you talk much to Jeannie, before you were both moved into the dormitory?"

She looked up at the ceiling, not at me, and said, "Not much."

"Where'd she work on-site before the welding?"

"She was a clerk."

"Like Belva?"

Nancy nodded.

"Did she work *with* Belva? Helping Mrs. Pinter?" I didn't know what I wanted to hear.

"No, she was assigned to the grade school office."

"That must have been kind of a nice spot."

"She was looking forward to the welding instead."

"Why?"

She looked me in the eyes, impatient. "It paid better. She wanted to be independent." Nancy put her hand in her pocket as she said this, like she was checking to confirm it was empty.

"Independent from . . . somebody in particular?"

Nancy looked over her shoulder as though we might not be

alone in the bathroom. Belatedly, I moved to each stall, confirming they were empty.

Nancy said, "It was none of my—"

"Was it a man who worked here?" I pushed.

"Are you trying to get me in even more trouble? I need this job, Jane. I need this money. Do you know what that's like? Trusting other people hasn't worked out so well for me."

"I know." I did. "Being falsely accused like that—it's crooked as a fishhook. I'm sorry *and* angry." I took a breath, hoping my sympathy would sink in. It was genuine. "But what if Jeannie didn't have a welding accident? What if what happened to her was connected to what happened to you?"

"What are you saying exactly?"

"What if somebody wanted to get rid of Jeannie and then needed to get rid of you? I mean maybe they're trying to get rid of all the lady welders, but maybe especially you if they think you talked to her a lot? If they think you know something."

"Do you think I'm in danger? Is that what you're saying?"

A woman dressed in housekeeping clothes, a big white apron and a name badge entered the bathroom, looking at both of us crosswise, as if we were malingering, before she headed to a stall.

I signaled to Nancy that we should leave. She collected her pail and mop and I picked up the scrub brush and pan and we went down the hall and out the back exit, stopping under a tree some distance away.

"I don't think you're in danger," I answered, barely above a whisper. "They tried to get rid of you by framing you, I think."

"And why would someone want to get rid of Jeannie?"

"You're in a better position to know than I am."

"I can't imagine even one reason."

"Is that true? Who was it, Nancy? Who was the guy she wanted to break free of?"

"I don't know that any of this is true at all. I'm just saying she needed money, that's all."

A curtain dropped over Nancy's face, and I doubted more pushing would part it. But I had to ask one more. "What did you call her?"

"Huh?"

"Did she give you a nickname or something she wanted to be called?"

"I called her Jean."

"Not too different than Jeannie, I guess."

"It was short for Imogen."

———◇———

CHAPTER TWENTY-ONE

DAY THREE

8 P.M., MONDAY, NOVEMBER 9, 1942

OWI Quonset
Lowe Town
Richmond, California

"Sandy," I hissed over the OWI telephone. "I need everything you can get about two people: Jeannie Lyons and Imogen Jenkins."

She was slow to answer. "Jeannie's the dead girl? Who's Imogen?"

"Remember? Three years ago, Lowe had an affair with his secretary, Imogen Jenkins, and then her really young husband died unexpectedly. Then Imogen disappeared, and Frank tried to find her because he thought Lowe was up to no good. But he never did find her."

"What does this have to do with our poster—"

"Jeannie Lyons is dead. But I'm sure Jeannie is Imogen Jenkins. She was working here as a clerk and trying to get on the welding crew. And then on the very first day welding, before the very first day, she's a dead body."

"Okaaaaaaay . . ."

I caught her up on my talk with Nancy. "But then there's this other thing. Jeannie was wearing a gold bracelet when she died with the initials *ILI*. So what's her real last name? Would you have somebody dig all this up, Sandy?"

She delivered irritation like static over the phone line. "You're getting kind of sidetracked because you have this thing against Adam and—"

"I know you think that, Sandy. But something's not right here. Jeannie's death wasn't an accident. I mean, why was she even welding when everybody else was celebrating before the shipbuilding started?"

I said that last bit too loud, and a reporter at the end of the table looked up. I hoped he hadn't heard much more than *before the shipbuilding started*.

"Okay. I'll have Wally nose around for Imogen Jenkins and Jeannie Lyons. But I don't know about the other part—about whoever doing bad welding . . ."

"I'll look into it. I'll find out what the problem was with Nancy's work, and whether it would be possible for somebody to fake welding problems after she'd finished. And I'll go back and see if I can get Nancy to tell me more about Jeannie. Imogen."

"Fine."

"Sandy, are you all right? You sound off."

"Oh, it's just Edward. He's awful. The worst. You saw him. Terrible mood. Doesn't want my help. It gives me a headache."

I paused. Since they'd married, I'd learned never to criticize Zimmer to Sandy. I used to speak my mind about him back when she was scheming to get the ring and elevate her status and her options. That was fine. But marriage canceled that privilege. After signing on the dotted line, she sure wasn't going to hear any complaints about the guy.

"I'm sorry, Sandy. What's happening? Is it about the printers?"

"No, actually he heard about me claiming to be associate publisher. For some reason that set him off. Ridiculous. But it's not just that. He's not acting like himself. Short with me, short with everybody, really. Acting really dark. I don't know."

"Well, do you think you should—"

"Listen, forget I said anything."

"Sandy, we're friends."

"And also I'm your boss."

"Actually . . ." Then I wished I hadn't said that one word.

"What, Jane?"

"I'm not implying anything."

"Really?"

"Okay, I'm saying you can do the work of publisher, you'd be an absolute bang-up publisher. But you're not the publisher. That's what I'm saying. Maybe he's not as cut out for it as . . ."

Sandy hung up.

STUPID, STUPID.

Ben was right.

Why did I keep doing this, offending the people who helped me? Had I learned it? Was it just in me, like it was in Momma, to insult people left and right? Or in this case, was it that I was a little bit jealous of Sandy—having no real love in my own life— and needed to believe that her marrying Edward had been a bad, pathetic decision? I had a lot of work to do on myself.

———◦———

CHAPTER TWENTY-TWO

DAY FOUR

7:30 A.M., TUESDAY, NOVEMBER 10, 1942

Shipyard School
Lowe Village
Richmond, California

Everything felt so urgent that at first I resisted my instinct to talk again to Louise, but finally gave in to it. I needed to make sure. I watched her at a picnic table with her kids, eating oranges and clowning. She looked younger than before. Her bandana was off, her hair dancing in the breeze. Her daughter snuggled under her arm, both of them comically making lips out of orange peels.

The boy was playing with a paper airplane, ignoring his sandwich.

Watching her with her kids, I knew she'd appeal to other women. She could convince them that they, too, could commit to work like this. Even if they were mothers, even if they loved their kids more than anything, that didn't have to stop them from doing this work. Being a mother didn't mean you couldn't also have other work you loved.

Momma'd worked in the fields when I was growing up, and she still worked, running the roadhouse with her husband now. There was no doubt she loved work.

I'm not saying she used to love picking tomatoes in 110-

degree heat. That would be stupid. But she did love being around other people, setting goals for herself, trying to break the goals—number of bags, weight of bags, coins brought home, corn, flour and beans bought with those coins, better tents or cabins at our Hooverville. She loved all of it. Maybe her work itself wasn't the best, but she valued herself as a worker. And I thanked God she didn't stay home with me instead of working, because we needed the money and I doubt I could have survived that much of her attention, truth be told.

I knew from experience a mother could be a worker and it didn't have to make her a worse mother, even though I also knew I hadn't been very good at taking care of my sister while also working at the *Prospect*. But that was me at nineteen. And I was selfish, with outsized ambition, a trait I happened also to like about myself.

Louise was an example who proved it was possible to be both, a mother and a worker.

I watched her do some kind of nursery rhyme clapping game with the little girl.

Then she pulled her hair back into its band and tied the bandana around it on top. Back to business. As the kids ran to join the lines of children outside their classrooms, Louise waved and then walked toward me.

"Surprise, surprise."

"You'd make a great poster, Louise."

"I told you that, day one."

"You're beautiful and confident and charismatic."

"Yes, I am."

"And the fact that you're a mother—that's even better. We need mothers to take these jobs."

"Yes, we do."

"But Louise, could anything in your history damage both the campaign and you?"

"That's not for me to say."

"Louise, what is it?"

"You're the reporter."

"Louise, did Inez Burns give you an abortion?"

Her little smile did not fade. "Do you have a problem with that?"

I'd be the world's biggest hypocrite if I had a problem with that. But others definitely would, and it was going to keep her from being the poster girl.

"Everybody would find out," I said.

"Mrs. Burns doesn't talk."

"Is she the only one who knows?" I thought of my mother, the only other person in my life who knew about my abortion. But then I saw, everybody who worked there knew about it too.

"No."

"Is your husband the other one?"

"No, he doesn't know." She stuck out her jaw.

OH, HELL NO.

"If he finds out, you're going to lose everything."

"Would I lose everything? Or would I gain something and lose something else?"

I asked her, "What would you be willing to lose? What would you choose to lose it for?"

"I could keep my kids. I wouldn't have to do everything in the conventional way. I could find a new way to do it."

I felt for her. She was courageous. She was ready to take a risk for what she wanted to do, a kind of woman I understood. But I just knew that people would uncover it. She'd regret the news getting out, regret her husband finding out. She would likely lose her kids. I could see all that spinning out of it. She'd probably also lose the acting, singing, dancing opportunities she longed for, too much tarnish on her. And the shipyard would lose the momentum it needed for this campaign. And that would splash back on me.

My heart ached for her.

She said, "I didn't figure you for the judgy type."

"I'm not."

"Okay, you really want to know?"

I nodded.

"So I was working at an insurance office, filing, my mother-in-law taking care of the kids. My husband's job didn't pay much. We *needed* my pay. We couldn't get by without it."

That sounded normal to me. Everyone I grew up around put the whole family to work, little kids included.

"My husband became resentful of me for working. I think he felt I was disrespecting him. And, I don't know, his acting that way made me actually disrespect him."

I knew from watching Daddy and Momma that a man could resent a necessary thing if it made him feel like less of a man. Louise didn't have to persuade me of this.

"I had an affair with an agent in the office. It wasn't much, but it was something for me. It was an escape."

That didn't sound great, but I understood. And I certainly couldn't judge someone for fooling around. But all those years of Daddy's infidelity? I had seen it create a distrust between my parents that never repaired, making whatever good things they had go bad.

"When I got pregnant, I took care of it. And I broke it off with the agent. My husband enlisted and I got a new job here. Started over. And that's why my husband doesn't know."

"But the agent does?"

"He paid for it."

That's only fair. She'd done what she ought to do about it. I sympathized. But it would be too damaging if it came out. "I'm sorry, Louise, you're not our poster girl."

CHAPTER TWENTY-THREE

DAY FOUR

NOON, TUESDAY, NOVEMBER 10, 1942

Yard Two
Lowe Shipyard
Richmond, California

Seventy-two hours after they'd begun building the SS *John Wesley Powell*, cranes as big as storybook dinosaurs hoisted the premade hull and laid it on the keel with almost half the ship, engines and boilers within. I don't know what I'd expected, but the fact that this ship was going to happen was a marvel of industry and planning.

Things were not running so smoothly for me. My favorite for poster girl was now struck off my list. Now back at square one, I had to consider whether I'd been unfair to Opal. Maybe she should go back on the list. She did have certain qualities we were looking for.

I stood watching her hold the welding rod, looking through the dense glass window in her hood at the blinding glare she ignited, maneuvering a continuous arc, leaving a path of molten metal. Taking what was originally separate and joining it through the momentary heat of the weld, a wondrous thing Opal was genuinely good at.

When she pushed up her mask for air, I jumped in.

"Impressive, Opal. Almost like art. Can I ask you a few questions?"

"You're full of questions."

"Where are you from?"

"Where are you from?"

"I'm from Texas."

"I gathered that."

I ignored the dig. I really tried to hide the accent but had never had much success. "What about you?"

"Outside Sacramento. You wouldn't know it."

I started to say I knew most fields and ditches surrounding Sacramento but stopped. That would confuse matters. She wasn't a migrant worker like we were. No telling what her opinions of us would be.

"Look, Opal, I think you might be a good fit for our poster girl. Can you tell me about your background?"

Opal took off her helmet, threw back her head, and laughed. This was the first time I'd seen her do it. She was really very pretty, which you could only know by watching her cheeks round up, squinting her eyes, her straight white teeth.

"Save your questions for somebody else. I am definitely not your girl."

Opal shook her head, amazed, and put her helmet back on.

She was reliable. She was smart. And unlike the powerfully female beauty of Louise or Nancy, Opal's was a competent beauty, like she made sure nothing was wrong with her. She would never let herself get fat, let her hair get messy or outdated, her clothes get inappropriate. She managed her appearance so well, she was every bit as beautiful as she needed to be, but no more so. Maybe that would be best for the poster girl. I wasn't giving up on the possibility.

I saw something else too: a shadow of loss. Even in childhood I could see that in people, especially men who'd fought in the First World War. They had a haunted look about them, a dimming of the light that used to shine in their eyes. Opal had that. Maybe that's why her laugh was a surprise. As efficient and on task as she was, her eyes made me think something was missing. It may have diminished her beauty, but it also made her more interesting, more sympathetic, more like everybody else.

Why was Opal so sure she couldn't be a poster girl? That bothered me. But below it was a much bigger question. The poster girl selection pool wasn't big to begin with, and now one of them was dead, one was no longer a welder, one had a shadow on her past, and this one was eliminating herself.

Why was I even trying to do this?

CHAPTER TWENTY-FOUR

DAY FOUR

4 P.M., TUESDAY, NOVEMBER 10, 1942

OWI Quonset
Lowe Town
Richmond, California

Sandy sat at the main table at OWI, ready to spring.

"Okay, okay, okay," she said as I took a chair across from her. "You were right."

"Jeannie is Imogen?"

She leaned in, looked left and right. "I won't go all the way. I don't know for sure if that's true. But I put Wally on the hunt, and there's no record of any real Jeannie Lyons nearby. And the last known address for Imogen Jenkins is in Lafayette, not far from Richmond. That was six months ago. Her lease ended and didn't pick up anywhere we can find, right about when Jeannie turned up here to work clerking. So I'm not saying you're right. I'm saying I can't find any reason why you're wrong. This is obviously nothing you have any business writing about without real evidence. So still focus on the poster assignment."

"Right. Yes. I will."

"And you'll forget about Adam Lowe for now?"

I grunted, "Yes." I don't think she believed me.

"What are you doing here?" I asked. "How about Zimmer? Everything okay?"

"Listen, I'm sorry about lashing out," she said.

"Me too," I answered. "So what about Zimmer?"

"He says he's fine. He didn't realize he'd been acting different. You know men."

"Not really."

"Well, he's in a dark mood and doesn't want me helping, so I figured I'd get out from underfoot."

"Are you . . . sleeping here?"

"No, of course not. I have my driver. I'll go home."

"That's great then." Sometimes I cut corners Sandy wouldn't approve. It would be inconvenient for her to stay here watching me.

She stopped to exchange waves with a friendly reporter from another paper.

Then she was right back to business. "So, what about Nancy, with the bad welding?"

"I didn't find out anything else yet. I will, I will. But I believe her. I think she probably did do good work, but slow. I think she's being framed."

"Framed? I don't know if anything will come of that, but it's not a good idea to pick her as our poster girl if somebody's going to leak that she's a terrible welder, kicked off the team."

"Agreed."

"So who?"

"Well, not Louise."

"Why not Louise? I like her for this. Pretty mommy."

"I can't go into it right now." Or ever, I thought.

"Who's that leave?"

"Opal or Toots."

"Give me a one-liner on each of them," she said.

I got a folder out of a box. "Here, look." I pulled out photos of both Opal and Toots, and she dragged them on the desk in front of her. I said, "Opal's smart, efficient, reliable, attractive, critical, bossy. And she thinks the poster girl is a stupid idea."

"Oh gosh, I'd throw it all away to follow her anywhere."

"Still," I said. "I could probably change her mind."

"Next."

I pointed to Toots's picture. "She's a charming, volatile, immature, funny kid sister who also doesn't seem to want to be a poster girl."

"She's pretty. Looks like we could amplify that with hair and makeup help. How old is she?"

"Eighteen."

Sandy slammed the table. "Let's go with Toots."

"I thought you'd say that, though if you met Opal, you'd probably like her. Hard worker. We have a couple days. Do we have to rush?"

"There's a lot to set up and it also sounds like we have prep to do with Toots, or should I say, Wendy."

I thought, *Yeah, lots of prep, including talking Toots into it.*

As I was repacking the box, Ben got in his dig.

THIS IS THE MOST IMPORTANT THING GOING ON?

Yes it is, I answered him in my head.

REALLY?

It is, for me.

THAT DON'T MAKE YOU LOOK TOO GOOD.

Everything was challenging enough without his interfering judgment. I turned my mental dial, silencing Ben's radio station in my head.

I didn't know a lot about Toots, but I did know she could be contrary. Not that she was a naysayer. But she wasn't someone you could predict. She might say yes to the poster, enthusiastically, if I asked her in just the right way, at just the right time. If I could make her see it as an adventure, she'd approach it boldly, cheerfully. She'd be exactly the right spirit for Wendy the Welder. Willing and able to take on a new challenge, to see the fun in it. She had the nerviness in her to be the right person and to look like the right person.

I'd do best to rush her with this idea, lifting her up on the tide of my enthusiasm. I had to make it exciting for her—and it *was* exciting. I felt buoyed by the optimistic task of persuasion, which I thought I was so good at. This would be no problem. No problem at all.

CHAPTER TWENTY-FIVE

―――――○―――――

DAY FOUR

5 P.M., TUESDAY, NOVEMBER 10, 1942

Women's Residence
Lowe Village
Richmond, California

I found Toots lying on her belly on the dorm room floor with a notebook and pencil in front of her. Bad luck. She appeared to have had an idea. A new distraction was a problem.

"What are you doing?" I asked.

"Making a list."

"A to-do list?" I asked apprehensively.

"Nah, just things I don't want to forget." She began to *rat-a-tat* her pencil on the floor, tapping a beat with her eyes closed.

"Are you thinking about taking a second welding class, when the contest ends?" I asked as gently as I could muster, herding her a little in the right direction.

"Um, I haven't decided." More pencil tapping. "I heard the electrical crew is interesting too. And they make a lot of money."

I breathed out my nose. "Thing is, Toots, it might be good just to choose it and do it. You know?"

"I can see that. But maybe that's a good reason to try the electrical too, so I can compare and then really choose." It was a strain to sound patient when I felt anything but.

"Toots, listen! Maybe you ought to focus."

"Well, Mother dear, I'll take that under advisement."

I could have said *touché* and given up, but oh no, not me. I barreled on. "Toots, I think you should be the poster girl. You can be an example to all the women out there who don't have something meaningful to do with their lives, who haven't found a way to be part of the war effort yet." I felt the truth of it, and it was good to believe in the rightness of this mission. I just needed to get her floating down the right stream.

"I'm not sure that's what I'm meant to do." Tendons strained in her neck as she looked up at me. "I was always dying to get out of my hometown, go someplace more exciting. Now I'm here, which seemed exciting, but it looks like I might get stuck here. I mean, how long would I have to be a welder, if I do the poster?"

I breathed relief. This I could answer. This I could fix.

"Toots, you could quit. Honestly. Let's make you the poster girl. Let's use your energy and charisma and charm and skill and all of it, to do a good thing for this cause. And you can have some fun while we're at it—think of all the things, the posing for the poster, the radio interviews, the meeting people. Then, a little while after that burst of activity, you can be done. If you decide you don't want to weld anymore, just quit, soon as the war's over. And it'll be over right away. You heard Lowe—lickety-split!"

The warmth returned to her face. "It doesn't have to be forever?" The promise of *temporary* might sell this to her. She was not a person who wanted to be locked down.

Her optimism and vitality—that's what the campaign needed. Her good cheer and humor and youth, all of it, would send the message we wanted to send, whether or not Toots was brilliant at welding or really intended to do it for very long anyway. As Belva said, we were just talking about an ad campaign.

My relief went beyond what it meant for this task because I knew it would be good for Toots too. Her daily life would be full of so much variety. She'd love it. Besides, she didn't take herself too seriously, didn't take anything too seriously. I'd be helping her to experience the pure pleasure and variety of existence. It was perfect.

"You'll do it?" I asked.

"What the hell." She grinned.

I threw my arms around her, feeling enthusiasm flow from me to her and back to me. I'd made this happen. It was a win for everyone. I'd be able to finish this project and focus on Jeannie, I thought.

CHAPTER TWENTY-SIX

DAY FOUR

6:30 P.M., TUESDAY, NOVEMBER 10, 1942

Lowe Town
Richmond, California

Heading to OWI to tell Sandy the good news about Toots, I saw Belva lock the door to Headquarters with something shiny and gold peeking out of an open purse slung over her shoulder. I sneaked up closer, following her as she marched. What was in her purse?

I got closer still and saw it was Mrs. Pinter's gold letter opener stand.

Belva had taken it off of Mrs. Pinter's desk. Did she think Mrs. Pinter wouldn't notice?

I thought about somebody entering Lowe's office in the middle of the night, interfering with my snooping. It had to be Belva.

She jogged toward the bus stop and climbed through the front door.

I hurried and hopped onboard in the back, sitting five rows behind her, trying not to breathe too hard as we rumbled off, seatmates chattering between our rows.

Shipyard workers got off at each stop.

Several minutes later, Belva rose for a stop in Oakland and

I followed, trailing her as she made her way up Seventy-Sixth Avenue to a tiny house set in a meadow, near Mueller's Dairy Farm, with fat black-and-white cows chewing and mooing all around. On the other side of the road were railroad tracks and, beyond that, some kind of marsh full of cattails and willows. Then a two-lane highway and the two hangars of the new Oakland Airport.

I watched Belva enter the pale blue painted front door of the house in the meadow.

WHAT NOW, DUMMY?

"Knock it off, Ben. I'm thinking," I said.

STOP THINKING AND START DOING—GET UP THERE!

So I approached the doorsteps, noting an elaborate metal rail and fence in the form of vines. I knocked tentatively on the door, hearing a murmur of sounds inside, people and music.

The door opened on an old woman with light chestnut skin like Belva's. She wasn't big, but she seemed to fill the doorway.

"May I help you?" she asked, with a French-sounding accent.

Belva appeared behind her. "What are you doing here?"

"Good evening." I nodded to the woman and then said to Belva, "I have some questions."

"Belva, who is this?" The elderly woman faced me, looking into my eyes, while asking Belva her question.

"No worry, Ma-Mère. Somebody from work."

"Is there trouble?" she asked.

"None at all, ma'am. None at all," I said.

Belva edged past the woman and came out to the porch, shutting the door behind her.

"What are you doing here?"

"You were right about Jeannie."

She waved me off the porch, and we walked toward the

fence that separated their yard from the cows. It was welded into the shape of a zinnia border. Like the flowers Momma always planted at our canvas Hooverville home.

"There was no real Jeannie Lyons around here, but there was an Imogen Jenkins, and the last place she lived was in Lafayette, nearby. Jeannie was Imogen, Lowe's former secretary."

"You followed me here to say that?"

ASK YOUR QUESTIONS. DON'T STALL.

"So Lowe brought her here, under a false name, set her up to work for his shipyard. Not exactly a sugar daddy move, is it?" I thought of the way he paid for Tommie's North Beach apartment, and her maid and travel and bar tabs and clothes. It didn't even look like he especially cared for Tommie, just that he owed her those things per their arrangement. "I mean, why wouldn't Lowe just set Jeannie up in some apartment where she got to paint her nails and listen to the radio all day?"

"Maybe she didn't want that. Maybe she just wanted a clean start, a new identity."

"You made it seem like they had a romance—"

"What if she didn't want that either, but she just needed a way to survive while hiding."

"What do you know about her?"

"Really, nothing. She was polite, which doesn't say much. But he did look at her special, anybody could see that. And I did see them talking privately, out on the yard before. That's it."

"You hinted her death wasn't an accident," I said.

"I'm not saying he killed her, obviously. Just that it was a strange accident. The shipyard has always had a good record for safety. People are saying that cable was cut clean. It's not the kind of thing that happens at Lowe."

"Which people are saying this?"

"Just people. Everybody."

"Belva, dinner!" the old woman yelled from the porch. Through the open door I could see bodies moving toward the food, could hear laughter and loud talk. There was a spicy smell, like sausage and garlic, and I wanted to follow it into the house.

"I appreciate your time," I said, wanting more of it.

She nodded and gave me a look—*anything else*?

ASK HER ABOUT THE STEALING.

"Do a lot of you live here together?" I asked instead.

"When people in our family move here from New Orleans, my grandmother provides safe landing, before they find their own place. I'm the only one living here with her now, but the others come around all the time. She makes a community of it."

"That sounds nice." I looked back at the house, which was a little in need of paint, maybe a new roof. But the porch was swept clean, no spiderwebs. It was really a place, solidly planted in its landscape, part of the meadow, the tracks, the airport.

"Did you do the welding?"

She looked away. "With my dad."

"It's special," I said. There was such artistry in it, on top of the obvious professionalism.

She turned back and I saw she was blushing.

"I better go in," she said. "Do you want to come? Are you hungry?"

I really did want to come in. I really was hungry.

GET IN THERE.

"Do you mind if I just use your restroom?" I hadn't seen an outhouse.

She looked into my eyes for several seconds. "That's fine."

I followed her back to the porch and into the door.

The kitchen of the small house had several tables pushed

together with old quilts thrown over their top, under platters of country food, sausage and rice and beans, pitchers of tea. Almost every chair was full. Everybody quieted when I walked in, the palest person in the room.

"She needs to use the restroom," Belva said. She pointed me in the other direction. "It's at the end of the hall."

"Thank you." My cheeks burned at the stares.

I walked the hallway. I quietly opened a door into what looked like it might be Belva's grandma's room. I opened a second, right next to the bathroom, and knew I'd found it. I closed the bathroom door, and entered the bedroom. Belva had taped sketches to the walls, designs of welded furniture. I wondered if she'd made these pieces or just dreamed of them.

Her dresser top was bare.

I opened a tiny closet and didn't at first see anything relevant.

Then, on the shelf over the clothes, I saw a woven basket and pulled it down.

Inside was the letter opener stand, my moleskin notebook and Jeannie's chain, left behind the night I'd snooped. There were also many other things, fountain pens, a handkerchief. Small things.

I felt Belva behind me before I heard her. The door closed.

"Well?" she asked quietly, without panic or accusation.

"Why do you do this?" I looked into the basket at her stolen booty.

Belva didn't shrink from the question. Her shoulders rose up, straightened.

"It's a way of correcting things. It's stupid, obviously. *Thank you for your service*? It's pathetic. But sometimes I just need to take something."

"Does it work? Does it correct things?"

"Clearly no. Every time I do it, I feel these little pinpricks in my hands and arms, this tingling like maybe I'm losing proper feeling in my limbs. I'm hurting myself, not them. They don't care about these small things."

I looked in the basket at the chain and the letter opener stand.

"They might care about some of them."

"Well then, if they do, I feel better about taking them."

I nodded. I understood. Sometimes a girl just needs to do a little damage.

"Are you going to report me?" she asked.

"No."

"Thank you."

"I should go," I said.

She nodded and I looked down at the basket, at my notebook, and Jeannie's bracelet, wondering if Belva knew I was the one who left them in the office, where she stole them.

I exited the house and walked to the road, where I waited for the bus, thinking Belva definitely knew and wondering if theft was her only crime.

A FEW HOURS later, I found Rupert where his OWI assistant had told me over the telephone to look, Jiggs Bar and Tavern at Thirteenth and McDonald, a noisy, welcoming spot for working men. The air was muggy, full of the yeasty smell of beer and perspiration.

I sidled up next to Rupert at the bar and ordered a Regal Pale Ale.

"Evening, young lady."

"Evening, Rupert," I said. "Glad I found you."

"On the hunt, I understand." His watery eyes and flaming cheeks suggested he was already soused. I didn't know if that helped or hurt my cause.

"I have our girl," I said.

"Hit me," he replied, wiping foam off his chin.

"Toots. Or, I should say, Viviana DeNatoli."

"What, the knuckle-sandwich girl from the rally?" His mouth gaped like a dead fish.

"You'll need to put that out of your mind."

"You've chosen that street urchin Toots as the face of the idea that good, all-American women should sign up to weld in the shipyard because it would demonstrate the purity of their patriotism, their newly war-forged womanhood?" He was far more voluble drunk.

"Where do you even get this stuff?"

"Thousands of people—and more via cameras—watched her insult the men she works with and threaten to fight them. You've convinced me we need a girl as our brand for this idea. Are you saying Toots-of-the-obscene-gesture is our brand?" His coat jacket slipped off his stool back, onto the beery wet floor.

"Well first, nobody's going to see that. She'll be cleaned up, looking the way we want her to look, so nobody's going to make that connection."

"The thousand guys she works with aren't going to make the connection?"

"But it's not going to make a difference. The picture matters more than their memory. Our picture will give them a new, different memory." I didn't know the scientific reason this was true, but I absolutely knew it was. The right picture would change their minds and their memories.

"Why can't we go with Louise? Louise is perfect. She'd

look amazing in the pictures." Rupert's eyes misted a little, as he wobbled on his stool. "Beautiful, married to a marine, a mother."

I thought, *And she really wants to be poster girl too.*

GIVE HIM HER TELEPHONE NUMBER. THAT'LL FIX IT.

Rupert continued, "She's the kind of person we want to bring in. And we want to convince guys to let their wives do this. She'll inspire all of them."

"Yes, sure, Louise is great, but she doesn't want it," I said, lying with my usual lack of compunction but a growing twinge of desperation. "She's worried about her kids—haven't you seen how the worry ages her? We don't want somebody looking haggard up there. That sends the wrong message." It didn't look like he was buying this, so I shifted. "She's under too much pressure. She wouldn't be available for the activities we want. She couldn't just leave her kids behind to traipse around to radio shows. Would you want to be responsible for separating her from her kids?" Now I was making headway. Rupert didn't want to separate her from her kids. "Toots will be better."

Still, Rupert's face was questioning. It would be difficult to wrest him from Louise.

I turned to a group of guys at the bar to my left. "Hey, what does it take for a woman to do the work at the shipyard, to succeed at it? Like as a welder."

One guy yelled, "Guts!"

Another said, "Backbone."

A third said, "Rhino skin."

I turned back to Rupert. "That's Toots. The superficial parts, we can fix. But she's got the nerve it takes to work at the shipyard. You can see it glowing right through her. You'll see it in the poster."

Rupert's left eye squinted, trying to see me better. Or maybe to see one of me rather than two.

"You are quite a person, sitting there in your borrowed welding uniform," he said, taking me in, his eyes resting on my waist and my thighs, under heavy work clothes.

OKAY, LEVERAGE.

He went on. "Maybe a single girl is better," he admitted. "But Toots is erratic. She could put the whole thing at risk. Let me talk to Lowe, see what he says. If he's okay with her, we'll do it."

"Talk with him right away then. We have to *jump* on this. The public attention is at an all-time high now. They're perfectly primed. If we lose their attention, we lose our chance."

"Right away," he said, though he avoided my eyes. "I'll check with a couple other people too."

"Rupert." I leaned into him. "You have to trust me! You have to trust yourself! You have to trust this idea."

His eyes bounced around the room while he thought, and then his gaze finished on me. This might take a little more effort.

I turned to the bartender. "Got any bourbon hiding back there?"

"Can you afford an old bottle? I got nothing new. Distillers are all using it for war alcohol, making gun powder. An old bottle will cost you."

I felt the money from Sandy in the *Prospect* envelope in my pocket, but I had no condoms or quinine sulfate or sponge. The bourbon better do the trick.

A FEW HOURS later, I got Toots up out of bed, out onto the lawn bench in front of the dormitory.

"So we're gonna call you Wendy the Welder."

Toots wrapped herself tighter in the quilt from her bunk bed. The wind whipped off the bay on our park bench conversation. "That's going to be my name?"

"You'll be Wendy DeNatoli. Wendy the Welder."

"What's my mother going to say about that?"

"She'll be proud to see you on a poster."

"Oh, that's what she'll be." Toots rolled her eyes.

"Is there some problem with your mother I need to know about?" *Please God, no more problems.*

"Is there a problem with yours?"

"Okay, right. I just mean, let me know in advance if there's anything we need to prepare for."

"You want my mother in the picture too?"

"Come on, Toots—Wendy—let's get the biography done."

"You're writing a book about me?"

"We just need a short description of your life to give the papers. Give me the who, what, when, where, and how."

"Say that again?"

"Where were you born and where'd you grow up?"

"Madison, Wisconsin."

"Town, city, country, farm?" I asked. Maybe I should have known what Madison was, but I'd never been there.

"Town. Not big enough." That fit.

"What about your parents?"

"Mom's a seamstress. She works out of our house."

"Okay, how about your dad?"

"He was a professor."

"A professor?" I lifted my pencil.

"What?"

"I don't know. That just surprises me." She didn't seem like a professor's kid.

"You mean how'd I turn out so uncultured?" She smiled her accusation.

"No, no. You said *was*." I tried to fix my insult. I wished I didn't always have so many to fix.

"He died when I was ten. In a train derailment."

My mouth dropped.

"He was on a research trip in Pittsburgh. The train jumped its track, plummeted down a high culvert, obliterated an electrical substation and part of a candy factory below. They say the train's coaches were just piled onto the street."

"That's awful," I whispered, and meant it.

"It's just history now. Mom and I made out all right. Don't make me tragic. Don't even mention it in the article."

Why did she see this as a secret? She and her mother had done nothing wrong, the reverse. They'd survived. Then I saw, it was about dignity, about not wanting pity.

"He's gone, but not really. Like with sewing? You can't see the bobbin, but you know it's there. Set too tight, the thread might snap. Set too loose, the thread might sag. Mom and I still have our bobbin set right. Maybe that's him."

They survived on a kind of magic, and it worked.

"Next question?" she asked.

"So if you get asked about your welding skills—"

"Should I pretend to have some?" She laughed.

"It doesn't really matter." We weren't going to put any small print details on the poster.

"It's funny," she said. "I'd been thinking a lot about quitting. I'm not good at welding. I don't love it, and there are plenty other things I could do."

"Just walk away? After the training and all?"

"Sure."

"When would you do that?"

"Right away. Not like the crew would miss my work. They'd probably finish faster without me in the way."

Toots didn't look unhappy about that at all.

"You can't quit yet," I said. "Just see this poster thing through. It won't take long."

"You promise it will be fun?"

"I do," I said. "You're going to love it." And in promising this, I wondered if I wasn't selling another tiny part of my soul.

CHAPTER TWENTY-SEVEN

---◇---

DAY FIVE

7:30 A.M., WEDNESDAY, NOVEMBER 11, 1942

OWI Quonset
Lowe Town
Richmond, California

The Lowe switchboard connected me to the *Prospect* switchboard, and I waited for a bit until Sandy picked up. "Columns are good. Love the pictures especially. But what about our girl?"

"I've got Toots."

"Toots the Welder doesn't sound too good. Did you tell her we're renaming her?"

"She's Wendy now. We've got two days. What do we do, in what order, to set this up?"

"Let me think."

I waited silently while Sandy thought.

"We need to get her the right clothes," Sandy said. "Nobody'll buy in unless she's wearing the right costume."

"She's already got welding clothes."

She sounded exasperated. "It's about color and pattern and texture and fit, dummy. She has to wear the manly clothes, but we have to fix it so they're not too manly. Emphasize the tidy and cheery."

Sandy wanted to remake Toots like Sandy as a welder. I had to admit that would sell the idea. "And we need the right setting, like at the edge of water, or next to the ship. And a hair and makeup person. One braid or two?" She rolled on. "And we need to announce a press conference, make sure everybody's there. We'll put it in the afternoon on Thursday, when they expect to finish off the ship thing."

I jumped in. "And we need to make a big spiel with the announcement. I've got to cinch Tommie." I had a pang. I hadn't gone to tell Tommie what I'd found on Lowe's desk about Frank yet. I had to do that. Had to.

"And Jane, we're going to need a good bio of Toots. It needs to be true, but cleaned up, according to what you've told me about her." Sandy sighed.

"It's done."

"And what about Hedda? She's going to swoop in for the press conference, obviously, act like she's the judge. What'll you do? Tell her it starts later, the next day or something? After the shipyard celebration, after our press conference has already happened? We'll let Tommie do it before Hedda gets there."

"That won't work. Don't you think she'll be there all day, the last day, with all the bigwigs? And besides, we need everybody's eyes on us. Listen, I have to figure out something here. I'll let you know."

I hung up, and immediately the phone rang again. "Jane here."

"Miss Benjamin, I've got Hedda Hopper on the line."

"Criminy," I muttered.

"Jaaaaaaane, Rupert tells me we have our Wendy. Well done! And you didn't even waste my time with the choosing. I certainly hope you've done us proud." Okay, so she'd decided to pretend we were working together. "I'll be there at nine Thursday for the end of the shipbuilding contest. We can go over the details. You'll get me materials, so I can talk the girl up? Explain my choice? Then we can announce Friday afternoon."

"Yes, the details aren't written up yet, but I'm working on—"

"And Jane, more important to you, I have a little offer to dangle."

I sat up in the hard metal chair.

"An offer?"

"I've just been on the telephone with Mr. Hearst?" Publisher of one of the most successful newspaper conglomerates.

"*The* Mr.—"

"That's the one. I'm not with his papers, but we do have a special friendship. I don't know if you know that."

"He has Louella Parsons," I said, wary about bringing up Hedda's arch enemy columnist. Everyone knew those two were out to get each other.

"Ugh. Right. Well, anyway, I was telling Will about you, how scrappy you are, what a comer, how you're on your way up and remarkably amenable and able to work with a person who has strategic imperatives in mind."

She was talking to William Randolph Hearst about me? She didn't even like me. My head began to whirl with questions. Why would she do this?

"I wondered aloud if Will might need an upstart like you on his staff."

"You said what? I mean, what about Louella?"

"Really, Jane, she's more of an albatross than anything else. At any rate, Mr. Hearst will be coming to our little unveiling event for Wendy."

"He's coming for us?"

"All right, I exaggerate. He was already planning to come in support of Mr. Lowe and the ship contest, but he'll also be there for our shindig. I told him he could meet you, then the two of you can talk about your future."

"Mrs. Hopper." I fairly stuttered. "I'm grateful for your passing my name along, but . . ."

"I won't be disingenuous, Jane. I hate Louella. I'm tired of her shenanigans. I would far more like to work with you over the bridge between our two news empires. Think about how you might feel to replace Louella for the Hearst newspapers, to work on a team with Mr. Hearst himself. Syndication, if your work pleases him. You can imagine how much more money that would mean. And how many more readers."

I could hardly breathe, but I *could* imagine. I'd been doing so for quite a while already. Syndication with the Hearst papers would be striking the mother lode. It would mean buying a house, a better car than my jalopy Ford. It would be proof of who I really was.

"Think on it, Jane. And I'll see you Thursday morning, for a Friday announcement. We can talk first thing, when I get there. But we'll postpone the announcement until Friday afternoon. The timing's better, after the build, before the launch."

"Thursday morning," I told her and hung up, my hands shaking.

I laid my head on my arms on the metal desk. Typewriters clacking. Guys yelling. The sound of machinery all around, inside and out. Whistles blowing change of shift. The only thing I really heard was me, telling myself, *You did it. You're getting what you most wanted. What you've earned.*

TWO-TIMIN' TURNCOAT.

Clam up, critic, I answered. *You try doing all the work for once.*

I'D LIKE THAT CHANCE, he said, pushing down on my remorse.

I put those thoughts away to start my column, though not about Toots. That one would come on the last day. Instead, I typed:

```
Nancy Moore isn't somebody you'd notice right
away.

She's every bit as pretty as any girl standing
at a soda fountain counter. But she isn't the
type to push herself to the front of a line.
Nancy is a gentlewoman, kind, generous, and
unassuming. A woman you might find in front of a
kindergarten classroom or a hospital bedside.
But that's not where she is. You might be
surprised to learn that the shipyard is a place
for every type of woman, even one who is top-to-
bottom girly, like Nancy. Are you somebody like
Nancy? Maybe you've got it in you to be a
patriot too.
```

And more like that.

I saw a *Prospect* copy boy dropping a delivery to the business news reporter and flagged him down.

"Call this in for me, kid, okay?"

"Yes, ma'am," he said, taking my piece.

My thoughts returned directly to Jeannie, and so I pulled her diary out of my pocket to read another entry.

I struggle in this stupid workshop with that awful man.

I don't want to forget, I was good at my job before. I know that clerking doesn't change the world. But I was good. My fingers flew on typewriter keys. I took shorthand as fast as any man could speak, and turned it into text with no errors. I scheduled everything, down to the last little item, so the executives never missed anything important. I was good. I was a detail person. I could be good again.

I can memorize new steps, practice them extra, stay as alert as possible to all the dangers. That's who I am, no matter what job I do.

That's what shores me up now, in spite of all the hurt. I've been good at work before, and I'll be good at it again.

Jeannie made me wonder, Was I good at what I did? What shored me up?

———◦———

CHAPTER TWENTY-EIGHT

DAY FIVE

9 A.M., WEDNESDAY, NOVEMBER 11, 1942

Bay Bridge
San Francisco, California

I steered my Ford through the mist blowing over the Bay Bridge. In the water below, two ferry boats shuttled workers and tourists back and forth, black freighters cut slowly across their wake, and the sails of tiny, shimmering yachts flew in between. Something about this mixed beauty and commerce settled me. I had made myself here.

Everything in the shipyard had been such a clanging rush, although it had also pushed me toward my own goal. I was executing a plan born of a chaotic situation, and now the prize hovered near my fingertips. I'd be rolling in dough. Have gobs of readers. I'd be a syndicated gossip columnist at the Hearst newspapers. I would be read everywhere.

Momma always said I was going to do something. She made it clear, she wanted to see me *earning* my way to a goal. She recognized my ambition, loved to see the effort when I turned it on. She didn't want to hear about my feelings. She never wanted that. *Just show me what you've done*, she said. She would love this, every bit of it!

But more, I felt good helping Toots to develop herself and share herself with the world, motivating her to greater personal achievement than she might have thought she was capable of. I wasn't going to disappear, doing nothing, being nothing, to nobody. And neither was Toots!

Then, as I exited the bridge, my thoughts started to itch and I began to pick at them, tearing off the corner of a scab.

Why would Hedda talk to Mr. Hearst about me? Did she actually see my talent? Did she hate Louella enough to do this to hurt her? Was it just a trick to help Hedda retain power, to stand alone, without Louella stealing occasional scoops and headlines? Did she know I'd been planning to ace her out of the poster girl pictures and headlines? Mrs. Burns said someone had been sniffing around about me. Was it Hedda? It had to be.

My car eased into Russian Hill traffic, and I pulled the scab all the way off. Would I do this to Sandy and the *Prospect*? If the Hearst papers and all they offered really were an option, would I betray the paper that started me and kept me? And my friend, who'd stood so loyally at my side? Sandy hated Hedda as much as Hedda probably hated Louella. Would I stab her in the back this way?

I THOUGHT THIS WAS WHAT YOU WANTED.

Please be quiet, please.

I liked things to be clear. I liked numbered lists, unpacked boxes, emptied trash. I liked typing *the end* at the bottom of my story. This was the reverse, everything sloshing and mixing together in my head. I began the search for a parking spot, which gave me enough time to beat myself up all over again. A Cadillac pulled away from the curb, and I lurched forward and back and forward again until I'd taken his place without further denting my Ford.

I slumped to Tommie's door, almost resentful I had to come share Lowe's information about Frank when so much was happening now at the shipyard.

I knocked on the door and Maria opened up.

"Thank God you are here, Miss Benjamin. Miss Tommie is a mess, absolute mess."

"What is it?" I said, assuming she'd been on another bender.

"Just go. She's had awful news."

I rushed up the stairs to her room, where Tommie lay sobbing on her bed.

"What is it?"

"Frank was on the Doolittle Raid."

"What?"

"Adam told me."

How much to confess? "What did he say that means?"

"Almost all the other men came home heroes, didn't they? Except the ones who are dead or captured. Adam told me he'd been doing research, calling the military people, to find out why I hadn't heard anything. He got somebody to tell him Frank was on a plane that went down, and we don't know exactly where he is." She sobbed with her whole body.

Tommie wasn't intellectual or studious, but she was a special kind of intelligent. She got some things fast, like in tennis. She had a kind of court sense about life. She knew what this news about Frank meant. And now her understanding delivered her to the worst-case scenario, and everything else crashed around her. She was estranged from the rest of her family. Frank was all she had. She was not going to be able to make this fact go away with more tennis, more parties, more magazines, more activity. This fact was immovable, unless Frank came home.

I sat on the side of her bed and patted her back. I didn't say anything. What could I say? I took her check from Lowe out of my pocket and set it on her nightstand and just kept patting. I didn't mention judging the poster girl contest. I felt sick.

———o———

DAY FIVE

1 P.M., WEDNESDAY, NOVEMBER 11, 1942

Yard Two
Lowe Shipyard
Richmond, California

It had to be Mickey who'd messed up Nancy's work. He had opportunity, skill, and motive. He was a woman hater. I'd known plenty of them, could see them a mile away. Most women could, except for the ones who couldn't. And that type gave me a pain. If they would just stop giving guys like Mickey and Farthing the time of day, the rest of us wouldn't have to put up with them. We'd all be better off.

I moved through Yard Two feeling mad and arrogant and ambitious all at once. Welding flames flared erratically around me. Enormous cranes moved pre-built blocks onto the hull of the ship almost fully formed. The workers looked anonymous and sexless in their compatible uniforms, helmets and masks and goggles over their faces.

So much had changed on-site since I had last been there, I had a hard time finding the pipe Nancy had supposedly ruined. I finally found it, inside a section of ship that had been preassembled and lowered over it and was now being welded down and secured.

I entered the dark and empty pipe. The external pounding on the ship echoed so that it felt like this liberty ship was already at war, or as if the war was coming from inside my own head. I rubbed my hand alongside the curved wall, unable to see anything. I took out my flashlight, holding it close to the steel wall, finding a seam and following it. I found a spot where I could tell a mistake had been fixed. The steel shone a brighter silver, and a pattern of infinitesimal scratches circled where the error had been ground down. I took two steps and found another ground-down spot. Then I took two more steps and found another. The spots were fairly evenly spaced. I dropped the flashlight.

Something loud, not like the pounding of machinery outside but like heavy footsteps inside the pipe came at me. The noise got close, its weight and hot breath slamming me against the wall of the pipe, jamming my cheek into the cold metal, pinning my arms behind my back.

"What are you doing in here, eh?" Mickey rasped. "Looking to ruin things, are you?"

"Get off me!" He was the killer and now he had me.

He gripped my arms tighter behind me. "Some kind of saboteur, yeah?"

"Let go of me! I'll scream." I knew that would be pointless. No one would hear anything inside this tube. Mickey had framed Nancy and killed Jeannie, and I would be next.

He grunted into my ear. "You got here and everything started happening. The girl was killed, the welds were ruined. You did it. What are you, a German?"

"You idiot," I groaned, my mouth against the wall. "No!"

Mickey threw me to the ground and turned a flashlight onto my face.

"Who are you working for?"

And God, the first thing I thought was, *I'm not sure.* The *Prospect*? Hearst? But that was only temporary confusion.

I pushed myself up to sitting. "I am what I said. A columnist. I'm trying to set up a poster girl campaign to get more women to work here. I'm the opposite of a spy. Why would you even say that?"

"What are you doing in here?"

"I wanted to see if someone could turn Nancy's good welds into bad."

"Well for Christ's sake, of course they can! YOU could!"

"I didn't! Jeez. Stop blinding me with that flashlight."

Mickey slid down the pipe across from me so that we were both sitting on the ground, his flashlight pointing toward the entrance.

"Why'd you fire Nancy if you knew it didn't have to be her?"

"I was mad, all right? We're working liking hell over here to break the record, win the war. We're all trying to make our mark! And besides, Jeannie was a nice girl! I couldn't just let that happen and not knock somebody's head over it."

Dammit. I believed him and even understood his getting mad like that. "Why'd you think it was me?"

Mickey dropped his head back against the pipe wall. "The cable wasn't nicked. It was cut."

I straightened. I knew that. People were saying it. But it was something to hear Mickey say it.

"I had my cop friend look at it because we'd been handling it all on-site, as an accident. There's a lot of welding deaths. This is wartime. This is one of the kinds of death that just happens now, so I'm not blaming Mr. Lowe. But I wanted to make sure, so I got my cop friend here from the city."

I wanted to ask the cop's name, but I thought it might slow his talking.

"He had the cable checked and told me it was a fresh, new cut. Somebody did it to electrocute her. I'm sure of it."

"When did you find this out?"

"Yesterday. After my shift. I headed over here to look around and saw you going in the pipe, and, well, you know . . . Sorry about hitting you so hard."

"Accepted."

"I thought you were a Kraut or something."

I winced. "We'll get who did this."

"I don't like you."

I GUESS YOU'RE NOT HIS TYPE.

"But I like that you don't let anybody push you around. No crying on deck."

Though, really, I felt like crying.

Mickey and I walked out of the pipe together, the right side of my face swelling, blood from a cut dripping onto my shirt. Workers turned to gape, central among them Opal, her eyes darting wildly between us.

"I'm okay," I said. "Mickey thought I was someone else, doing something I wasn't doing," I reassured her and the rest of them.

People looked from me to him and back again.

"Just a mistake," Mickey barked. "I got her—everybody, back to work."

Opal grabbed my arm and whispered, "Do you need help? What happened?"

Her concern made my face hurt more as I realized how bad I must look for someone as industrious as Opal to stop work for me. I gripped her arm back. "I need to talk to you."

"Mickey, I'll get her to the field hospital to see if she needs stitching up."

"Now look," he said.

"Don't worry. I'll get her in and out. No fuss."

And Opal took my arm in hers and walked me through Yard Two, everybody staring as we went. I was surprised how dizzy I was, how much I needed her support.

"I don't want this to mess you up," I said, meaning it.

"Not at all. We'll get you taken care of, tucked in, and I'll get back to the yard in no time. Things like this, you can't ignore. Things like this can scar."

I recalled the injuries I'd suffered in the past few years, and how bad I'd been at taking care of them. I'd put them away to deal with later. Maybe it had been important to take care of myself, but it wasn't urgent. What was urgent always took precedence with me. Maybe that explained a few things.

"So Mickey did this?" She looked at me with eager empathy.

"It was a case of mistaken identity. I don't blame him."

"Who did he think you were, to do this to you?"

"Maybe a German spy." I laughed, though Opal looked alarmed. "I know, I know. He thought I was trying to damage the liberty ship by killing off workers, ruining morale or something. He said things started happening when I got here."

"I never would have figured Mickey as having such imagination," Opal said.

"I know. He can seem like a potato on broad shoulders, but he's apparently got some sort of brain." I right away felt bad about saying that, since I'd decided I liked him now.

"What do you think of his theory?" Opal asked.

"Ever since you and I were there with Jeannie's body, I've been wondering if he did it." Only an hour ago, I'd been sure about that. Now I cringed, wondering what else in this whole convoluted series of events I was wrong about. I added, "But now I'm sure it's not him."

"But you think someone actually did it? It wasn't an accident?" She slowed down our pace. The field hospital stood just ahead.

"I don't know for sure," I said, doling information out more subtly than I wanted to. Something about my injury and Opal's kindness right now made me want to share more. She was the leader of this group of women, and she had sympathy for me. That meant something, I'm not sure what. I didn't have much to offer. She didn't want the poster gig. But I did have information, and it was tempting to share it. "Mickey said the cable definitely wasn't nicked. It was cut. Intentionally."

Opal stopped. "It wasn't carelessness? A poorly tended cable? Because—"

"The police had a look and said no."

"What were the police doing here?"

"Friend of Mickey," I answered, wondering why she thought the police were the strange part.

"And who would want to kill Jeannie?"

"That's the question."

She leaned into me. "You know, Jeannie wasn't who she pretended to be."

"Who was she then?"

"I've heard she was Lowe's former lover."

"Do you think it was former?" I asked.

"How would I know? I don't know all her details. I'm not some gossip."

———————○———————

CHAPTER THIRTY-ONE

DAY FIVE

4 P.M., WEDNESDAY, NOVEMBER 11, 1942

Field Hospital
Lowe Town
Richmond, California

The doctor shot me full of anesthetic and stitched up my cheek, giving me one more barrier to conventional beauty. Nothing serious, just another scar. I passed out in the hospital bed and slept, for the first time in three days, without dreaming. When I finally blinked my eyes open, there sat my nightmare, Adam Lowe, in a chair at the side of my bed.

I gasped. I had no control over that reaction.

"You aren't going to sue me, are you?" he said, leaning back in his chair, bouncing one leg crossed over the other.

"Excuse me?"

"Say I'm liable for your workplace injury?"

"I currently have no plans of that nature."

He chuckled. "Please let me know if you change your plans. I'll want to alert my lawyers."

"Probably a good idea. Why are you here?"

"Tell me what you've learned at Lowe Richmond," he said.

Some horns and whistles went off in the background, and Lowe's forehead wrinkled. He looked toward the window, but nothing was visible. "Those sounds are getting me. Like Pavlov's dog," he said. "So, come on, what have you learned, other than not to wrestle with my foreman?"

I ignored his question and returned to mine. "Why are you here? What are you doing in that chair next to my bed, when I'm sure you have more important things on your calendar?"

"I wouldn't be so certain of that." He half smiled and my stomach clinched. He was so handsome, the kind of guy who became more and more so, growing craggier over time. "You're still a friend of Tommie's?" he asked.

"More or less."

He laughed. "It is hard to know where you stand with Tommie. So you're here to advance your own success by advancing my success," he continued. "Do I have that right?"

I got hot, mad for making myself a tool to advance his success. "I guess, accidentally."

"Someone broke into my office, looking for something or other. You know about that?"

Belva must have told him. I felt the instinct to lie but controlled it. I'd been raised by liars. I knew the best tactic: tell a slice of the truth.

"Tommie sent you a letter returning your check. She changed her mind. I broke into your office to get the envelope with the returned check for Tommie."

"Tommie changes colors hourly. A human sunset. And while you were there . . . ?"

He'd already told her about Frank, so I could give that up too.

"I saw your notes about Frank. Being missing in action from the Doolittle Raid."

Another siren screamed out the window. Lowe got up,

looked outside for a minute, and then returned to his chair, looking troubled. "I told her."

"I know."

"Though I didn't tell her everything."

"What else is there?"

"I explained about the raid, that the bombers were supposed to head for unoccupied China after dropping their load. There's more."

My hands clasped in my lap.

"Vladivostok was much closer to Japan, but the Russians wouldn't agree to let them land there. So China was the only alternative. If they couldn't make it to the Chinese coast, they were supposed to head west, ditch their planes at sea, and make their way to shore in rubber boats."

I sat upright, giving my lungs more room to do their work.

"Frank's plane was short of fuel and forced to land near Vladivostok. He and his men are being held prisoner."

I hadn't considered that word yet, *prisoner*.

"Since April?"

"Seven months," he said.

"What's the air force doing? They can't just leave them there!" This came out as some kind of accusation.

"I haven't been told of their plans."

"Have you been told he's alive?"

"No. Nor if he's been tortured."

I turned and vomited over the side of my bed, my head pounding.

Lowe brought me a towel and then he called out the door for a nurse, telling her as she cleaned up, "This isn't her first concussion."

The nurse left to fetch supplies.

"Is there anyone you can call?" I heard the begging in my tone.

"I'm making the calls I can make. I just wanted to let you know. I haven't shared this with Tommie because I'm not sure she can handle it."

"That may be true, but, even so, do you think it's right to withhold that information?"

"I guess we all make that kind of decision all the time, don't we? When to talk, when to keep quiet. The preeminent example of your profession, Mrs. Hopper, likes to reveal things she oughtn't and to conceal other things."

I thought about Hedda's recent column, in which she hinted that Lowe was having workplace affairs, in the same paragraph where she mentioned his wife as a carefully placed afterthought.

"She's famous for making those decisions," I said.

"I am sure she must have her own way of judging what purpose she achieves by talking. I imagine you've given some thought to that."

"I have."

The nurse returned with a compress and a cup of ice. Several more sirens screamed by the building. The sound brought me back to the raid at Mrs. Burns's clinic, at the feeling that police could mean more trouble than help.

Lowe stood and looked out the window again.

I screwed up my nerve and asked, "Who is I.L.I.?"

He returned to my bedside, ashen. "So you *have* learned some things besides welding. Where's the bracelet?"

"I'm not sure. I saw it on the floor in this hospital."

"It's not who. It's what. *I.L.I.* means 'I love Imogen.'"

Something collected in my throat. He was being more honest with me than I was with him.

164

He said, "I'm glad you're all right. And that Tommie got her check." Then he left my room.

I wouldn't have known what else to ask him right then anyway.

Frank had to be saved. In comparison, who cared about my stupid job? Who cared about Jeannie or any of the welding women right now? Why was any of this my business? Lowe was the best person Tommie and I had for saving Frank. That's what mattered.

It wasn't like Frank and I had some grand affair. We had sex one time, my first time. It was the opposite of spectacular because both of us were blotto after a long night of drinking. I'd been at some kind of high point where I thought I could take over the world, so I just decided to fall into bed with Frank. I didn't regret it. I'm glad I tried it for the first time with a pretty good guy, except for the part about being one of those sorry sacks who gets pregnant after having sex only once in her life and then having to make the acquaintance of Mrs. Inez Burns. I wasn't sorry about that either. Momma was right. It had to be done. For me, for Frank, and for the child. I would make a terrible mother.

The thing that dangled over me, though, was that having the abortion made me think I ought to make my life worthwhile. Somehow, the possibility of Frank dying now felt terrible. Events from my past constantly blocked me from progressing. Even Lowe was throwing things off for me, seeming a little heroic, or at least human.

The wail of an isolated siren escalated into a chorus, bringing me back to the present.

———o———

DAY FIVE

6 P.M., WEDNESDAY, NOVEMBER 11, 1942

Yard Two
Lowe Shipyard
Richmond, California

I didn't get to Toots until she was gone.

Not because the hospital wouldn't let me go, but because I was so woozy after my injury and medication, I struggled to dress and put on shoes. When I finally got down to Yard Two, source of the dreaded sirens, throngs crowded around a tall scaffolding.

"What is this?" I asked.

The guy next to me said, "She fell."

"Who fell?"

"Toots."

"Is she hurt?"

"She's dead."

"No, she's not! No, she's not! She was just having her picture taken. She wasn't working this shift. This doesn't make sense!"

He pointed up high, to a scaffolding, metal dangling. "They were taking her picture up there."

I looked around for Sandy and found her. "Whose idea was that? She wasn't supposed to do that!"

Two men in emergency gear passed with a stretcher, a tarp over Toots.

I saw Sandy surrounded by officials. I saw Louise and Opal, their arms around each other's shoulders, eyes red, faces wet.

I rushed them. "What happened?"

Louise said, "They were trying to get pictures of her spot-welding up on the exterior, and she fell. We didn't see it, but we heard it."

"What did you hear?"

"She screamed, obviously, what do you think?" Opal barked.

"I need to know what happened."

"She fell, Jane, she fell!" Louise sobbed.

"Most common welding death," said another man passing behind me. "A fall from on high."

The ambulance sped away, Toots loaded into the back.

I ran to Sandy, who threw her arms around me, crying. "Oh my God, Jane, it was terrible!"

"Why was she up there?"

"It was her idea! We'd taken all these shots down on the deck, and then she said she wanted to do one up high, show the excitement, she said."

I grabbed Sandy's shoulders with both hands. "Are you sure it was her idea? Could it have been anyone else's?"

"Sure, it could have—I don't know." Her shoulders shook with her sobs.

"Who was she talking to?"

"Everybody! She was talking to everybody! Ask Opal if she heard anything. She was by Toots's side the whole time. She would have heard."

I waited a minute, thinking.

"Tell me exactly what happened."

"Lots of people were talking to her—they were excited about the poster. They liked Toots."

"I know. What about Opal?"

"She stuck close, helping, moving some people away, clearing a path for us to take the photos. She even helped the photographer up on the scaffold, below where Toots was. Opal held some of the photographer's equipment. She almost fell when Toots did. She was very devoted up until the last."

"Devoted," I echoed.

———○———

CHAPTER THIRTY-THREE

DAY FIVE

9 P.M., WEDNESDAY, NOVEMBER 11, 1942

Sea Cliff
San Francisco, California

I was in no shape to drive, but I had to go. After the sirens had stopped and the yard cleared, I forced my eyes wide open driving back over the bay, gripping the wheel, needing desperately to get to someone who might take care of me.

Momma's huge, Italianate home sat in the most coveted block of the most exclusive San Francisco neighborhood. Perched literally on a cliff, it overlooked the Golden Gate Bridge, San Francisco Bay, and the Pacific Ocean. It had four floors, five bedrooms, six bathrooms, solariums with arched windows from which you could see porpoises, even an occasional whale. Obviously I hated it. It was too perfect. And where did they get the money? I knew their roadhouse at the beach didn't pay for this. But Momma and Jonesie didn't share the details. I came here regularly anyway to see my sister, whose presence made up for the wrongness of the house.

Elsie was asleep when I got there, Jonesie was working at their roadhouse, and I was glad. I just needed a momma, even *my* momma.

She must have seen how bad it was because she managed to do all the right things. She settled me on the couch under a blanket with a hot toddy, heavy on the bourbon. She controlled her usual instinct to push and boss me, and instead just listened to me weep. Maybe all this money they apparently had now made it possible for her to be a better mother. Maybe.

After I'd worked my way through the basics of what had happened, I finally got around to the core of it, telling Momma through tearful croaks.

"This is my fault. I pushed Toots to do this whole stupid poster girl thing. She didn't want it. She'd be alive if I hadn't pushed her so hard, telling her how much fun she was going to have."

That's what made me hate myself.

Momma spoke up. "Wasn't that the truth? Wasn't the poster a chance to do something special she hadn't done before? The column in the paper made it sound like she liked adventure. It's not like you lied to her."

"But I was pushing her." I gagged on sobs. "I mean, it's not like I haven't done that before." I didn't want to go on but felt the pressure to say it. "Sometimes it's so hard to stop myself from persuading somebody that something will be good for them when really I'm pushing it because it would be best for me."

Momma sat down, pulled my feet up onto her lap, and rubbed my arches.

I saw what I'd done, like the frames of a movie, flying by my eyes, all the convincing I'd done, while Toots resisted, instinctively knowing she shouldn't do what I suggested.

"I'm sorry this happened to Toots. And that this has happened to you."

She didn't tell me what it meant, didn't pretend to be some

oracle who could help me fix things. And that was what I needed. I just wanted to feel bad in the presence of someone on my side. That's what Momma did for me that night. She gave me room to grieve and reflect.

Though she offered a guest bedroom, I preferred the big couch in front of the windows, so she made a bed of it and tucked me in under a fluffy down comforter and I shocked myself by falling right asleep, the sound of foghorns slipping into my dreams, reminding me I had work still to do, though the nature of the work had changed now.

I woke in the morning when Elsie hopped on the couch and squeezed my head in her warm, chubby arms. "Sissy! Momma didn't tell me you were here!"

"I came in late, then I spent the night so I could see you before kindergarten, girly."

We hugged each other hard. Elsie's hugs were the most healing things in my life.

She pulled away. "Will you be here after school too? Help me with my alphabet?"

It was so tempting to stay there on that couch, waiting for Elsie to come home from school. I looked up at Momma, whose face revealed nothing. Anything was possible. I wouldn't be judged, except by myself.

"I don't think so, Elsie. I have work to do."

"Work, work, work. So boring, Sissy."

I forced a smile for my sister. "It's never as interesting as you are."

"Will you promise to take me to Playland-at-the-Beach when you finish?"

"I do promise. It's the best thing on my calendar."

Elsie squeezed me again, a long one, like she knew something was wrong. Then she let go and ran to the kitchen for oatmeal.

Momma stood before the windows, looking out at all that blue, the vast expanse that only the very rich can horde in their homes.

"Have you got some kind of plan?" she asked.

"Not yet. But I have to get back to the shipyard. I guess I'll figure it out there."

She nodded, her back to me, then spoke. "I'm not the momma you might have wanted, or needed."

I didn't know if she expected me to interrupt and disagree. She laughed when I didn't and turned around to look at me.

"But I want to say I could not be prouder of who you are, what you've made of yourself, starting from scratch. You really have done a lot, Jane."

She never said things like that. She always said she expected me to do something, never that I'd done it. My eyes refilled with tears.

"Problem is," she continued, "in order to be someone who really does things, you're going to make mistakes. Terrible mistakes. It can't be avoided. I'm not saying to discount the tragic mistakes. I'm saying you've got to know they'll come and you've got to get over them. You're already so much better than me. You have the grace to admit when you've done something wrong. It's taken me a dang sight longer to learn to do it."

"Is that what you're doing now?"

"It is."

I pushed up off the couch and took my tiny mother in my arms and hugged her as hard as Elsie hugged me and Momma hugged back.

I didn't want to ever leave that moment. But it was time to cross the bay again. Time to find out whether I'd pushed Toots too far or whether someone else had made the real push.

CHAPTER THIRTY-FOUR

DAY SIX

9 A.M., THURSDAY, NOVEMBER 12, 1942

Yard Three
Lowe Shipyard
Richmond, California

I found them all on the dock at the new Yard Three, not yet in use.

Louise dangled her feet over water. Opal and Nancy slumped on the deck.

Lowe had paused work that morning on Yard Two, to let the police in, and my roommates sat on Yard Three, close but apart from the place where it happened.

Louise jumped right in. "It wasn't your fault," she said.

"If I hadn't pushed her—"

"Then what?" said Louise. "The poster has nothing to do with her falling from a scaffold. Welding high up is her actual job. This isn't about you. Go ahead and feel bad, but feel bad about her, not you!"

"I'm not feeling bad for myself. I'm feeling like I pushed her too hard. Maybe if I hadn't . . ."

"The truth is," Opal stepped in, "we're the newest welders on the yard, most likely to make a mistake, a fatal mistake."

"So she climbed up on that scaffold to do welding photos, and it was her idea?" I asked.

"How should we know?" said Nancy, as if I'd accused her of something.

I heard someone approach, turned and saw Belva.

"May I join the wake?"

Opal looked at her suspiciously.

Louise nodded to Belva.

"It could have happened to anybody," Belva said. "Just a slight misstep. It *would* have happened to somebody if it hadn't happened to Toots. Sounds like there was something wrong with the scaffold."

"So it wasn't just a balance thing? It was a problem with the scaffold?" I asked.

"That's what they're saying," she answered.

I felt my face getting red, and thought the tears might come again.

"So you're feeling guilty." Belva stated the obvious.

"Are you accusing me? What right do you have to imply this was my fault?" I couldn't stop myself from lashing out.

"We all play our roles."

"What are you saying?" I yelled.

"Listen, ladies," Nancy interrupted. "There's no need to—"

"What are you saying?" I repeated. "What role do you think I'm playing?"

Belva said, "You're like some movie star, or a flyboy, a grandstander. You don't even see the risks of what you're doing. Sometimes people get hurt. Like Toots. I'll bet it happens all the time around you, and you never see it coming."

"Shut up!" My anger flared because she was right. People near me did get hurt.

Louise came to my side, sat right up next to me, putting her hand on my back.

"So maybe that's me," I said, "but what are you? Huh? You're a thief!"

Belva blanched and I immediately regretted saying that. Her stealing those trinkets didn't mean anything other than making tiny little shifts that could help her through the night.

Her face shifted, as she made a decision. She said, "Listen, things don't make sense. Why are so many things going wrong around here? The accidents, equipment failures. There have been more than you know. I deliver the weekly accident reports the government requires. And I read them."

"What happens with those?"

"Nothing that I've witnessed. Seems like they need the forms filled out, but I don't know if anybody reads them. Anyway, I figured you might be part of the problem," Belva said.

"Why would you think that?"

"I believe you've done some after-hours snooping." So she did know. "Besides, the minute you arrive, things start happening."

Just like Mickey said.

I stood up, my back to the bay. "I got here exactly when the speed contest began and the women started welding. Of course things started happening then. But you agree Jeannie's death and Toots's death and the mistakes are all part of the same thing?"

"I don't know, I don't know."

There was enough *I don't know* to spread thick all around us, but one thing I now did know: my goals here were stupid and harmful. I didn't care anymore about this whole poster thing, I didn't want to betray Sandy, and I didn't want anybody else dead or hurt. And it *was* my fault. "Toots told me she wanted to quit. I talked her into staying until the poster thing was done. If not for me, she'd have been on a bus or a barstool instead of in the morgue."

"Hindsight." Opal wrapped her arms around her bent knees.

I wanted to quit too, go back to my solitary railcar home and drink myself to sleep all day. I couldn't do this place right, and I didn't want to do it one minute longer. Mine was the worst kind of failure, the kind that killed.

"It's all over," I said. "They're going to shut you women out. It looks like having you here is putting the whole shipyard mission at risk."

Belva disagreed. "You're not out of options. None of us are. I'm not saying your stupid poster thing is going to work. I'm saying maybe the women don't have to get kicked out of the shipyard. Maybe we can stop whoever's doing all this damage."

"How do you suggest we do that?" asked Opal.

"I don't know," said Belva. "I'm no hero."

They all looked at me for a plan, but I had nothing to say. Not yet.

CHAPTER THIRTY-FIVE

———•———

DAY SIX

11 A.M., THURSDAY, NOVEMBER 12, 1942

Yard Two
Lowe Shipyard
Richmond, California

The yard swarmed with non-Lowe professionals. When Jeannie died, it was only the field hospital workers tending her. This time they called in the Richmond Police.

They cordoned off the area around the scaffold Toots fell from. Blood stained the concrete. Some of them worked around the deck; others were climbing on a police scaffold that had been erected next to the original. I watched and took notes as they did their work.

When one guy climbed down, I approached.

"Jane Benjamin with the *Prospect*."

He looked at me, suspicious.

"What have you found out?" I asked.

He took off his cap and rubbed the top of his head, his eyebrows furrowed. He was one of those young guys who looked like an old one. Like a bloodhound.

"Not for public consumption," he said.

I gave him my card. "I won't put anything in the paper before you say it's okay. You can call and leave a message letting me know when and if it's okay. If you never tell me okay, I'll never put it in the paper."

"Says here you're a gossip columnist."

"I know. I'm asking you to trust me anyway. I want to earn your trust. I'm not a bad guy."

He put his hat back on, straightening it, and sighed.

"Doctor says she definitely died from the fall, cracked her skull, intracranial bleeding. Everybody around here's saying a fall is the most common cause of shipyard welding death. So it all works. Except for the scaffold. The bar she stood on broke clean off. I can't see why the metal would have failed. It shouldn't have failed."

I thought of Mr. Farthing, telling me it wasn't difficult to ruin a perfect welding seam, just like cutting open an old injury.

"Thank you. Please let me know if and when I can use this information."

"All right, Miss Benjamin."

"Is Miss DeNatoli at the field hospital?"

"She's at Providence Hospital in Oakland."

So they took her out of Lowe's hands.

CHAPTER THIRTY-SIX

DAY SIX

1 P.M., THURSDAY, NOVEMBER 12, 1942

Headquarters
Lowe Town
Richmond, California

I told Belva I needed to see Lowe and he let me in immediately.

"Close the door. What is it?"

He didn't sound or look like himself, with stringy hair and a wrinkled shirt. The room was stuffy, like he'd spent the night at his desk and not left yet.

"I do have questions." I felt no fear of him at all; in fact, I felt the reverse, like I had the power in the room. "They say Toots is at Providence Hospital."

"Yeah, and the Richmond Police are tramping all over everything here."

"Did somebody call them right after it happened?"

"*Somebody*? I called the police and Providence Hospital, soon as the field hospital docs told me about her head. Dammit, what else could I do? Trying to get these ships out to service as fast as we can, bodies are piling up everywhere on battlefields— that seemed like the most important thing. Now women's bodies are piling up on my shipyard! I can't let that stand!" His voice cracked, and he pinched his brow with his fingers.

I struggled to keep up, to reorganize what I thought.

"What did you think was happening before, when Jeannie died, and what do you think is happening now?"

He looked up, surprised, as if these questions were not what he expected.

We were surprising each other.

"I need you to leave now. I need the professionals to do their work, and I don't want to talk to a gossip columnist. I'm sorry."

He pointed at the door.

Still, I asked, "What's the difference between now and then?"

"Go!" he yelled, and I went.

Belva was standing a few yards away, nothing in her hands, just waiting.

I closed the gap between us and whispered, "We need to make plans."

She was a thief. And she didn't appear to trust me. But I tend to turn to skeptics.

"Listen, Belva, I have five thousand character flaws. I know that."

"Why would you—"

"I could tell when you stood on your porch, with your grandmother. There's something solid about you. I know you're smart. You've been paying attention. I just trust you. That's all."

"And you need something in here." She looked around the office.

"That too," I admitted.

"Mrs. Pinter's going to be back from lunch soon, the rest of them too. You need to get out."

"You need to take a lunch break," I answered.

"We can't let anybody see us together."

I grabbed a fountain pen off of Mrs. Pinter's desk.

"Tell me where." I held out my open left palm and handed her the pen.

Belva uncapped it, held my hand steady, and wrote on my palm, *Leo's Defense Diner—501 Cutting Blvd.* She pressed too hard on the final *d*, piercing my skin, bringing up a drop of blood. I wiped it off the address, took the pen and pocketed it.

"Half an hour then. I'll get the others there too."

"Which others?" She frowned.

"Don't worry." I understood that was underwhelming comfort.

"What is it you think we're going to do?" she asked.

"The plan's got two parts. The part we share with the group, and the part only we know about. I'll tell you the second part after."

———o———

DAY SIX

2 P.M., THURSDAY, NOVEMBER 12, 1942

Leo's Defense Diner
Richmond, California

Peggy Lee's jazzy number "Why Don't You Do Right" scratched on the diner's jukebox, her cynical voice carrying an edge through our conversation. The crowded lunch counter faced the street, jammed with shipyard workers, nobody in suits and ties. There were whites and Negroes from both shifts, since work had shut down on the shipyard today with plans to start up again with night shift at five o'clock. We had not an inch to spare in that diner, everybody eating, talking, subconsciously aligned to Peggy Lee's beat.

Sandy had arrived first and got us the one big table in the back corner, where we stood the best chance of our talk being muffled by kitchen sounds. We ordered hot dogs, corn dogs, grilled cheese sandwiches, and sodas. Then we settled in to plan.

"We'll do this on tonight's shift. Everybody'll be on the yard or nearby. They think with everybody working they might finish tonight."

Nancy said, "With Toots dying? Do they think everybody's going to be okay working there? I mean, does it even seem safe?"

Opal said, "I've heard people talking." She looked around. "They're spooked. Not trusting Mr. Lowe to take care of conditions. I'm wondering if it will open up again at all, if it *should* open up."

I felt an unfamiliar urge to defend him. "I talked to Lowe today. He seemed ripped up by this and passed all the investigation of Toots's death off to the police and the hospital in town, so he seems to agree with the seriousness—"

Louise said, "I don't know. It's hard to keep up with guys like that. Is he playing some other level of chess or something, to make the money he wants to make? Maybe we just can't properly interpret what he's doing."

I didn't know the first thing about chess, but I had no choice but to play. I pushed on.

"Sandy, you're going to make a show of playing up our poster contest, like we talked about, like it isn't over. Show up with the photographer, take pictures of the ladies, start your bossiness. Attract attention to what you're doing."

"Got it." Sandy was efficient as ever but flatter than usual, which made sense given she'd been with Toots when she died. I needed to talk to her in private, make sure she was okay, but for now it was best not to have the conversation. I didn't want to lay everything on the table.

"So far as everybody knows, Opal, Louise, you're the last two left in competition for the poster."

I looked at Nancy apologetically, then continued. "Do what you'd normally do. Weld as well as you can. Act like that's the only thing going on. But keep your eyes open and interfere if anything wrong starts to happen."

Opal and Louise looked askance at each other, tense at their uncomfortable alliance. I saw now how little they liked each other.

"Belva and I will search Headquarters, see what we can find

out, any kind of notes by Lowe. He scrawls over everything. He definitely clammed up when I was asking him questions today. There's something he didn't want to share."

Belva spread her fingers on the table, wiping off invisible crumbs.

Opal asked, "So you're thinking he was part of what happened to the girls? Or that he's covering up something somebody else did?"

"He loved Jeannie," I said. "He wouldn't have killed her. Besides, it works against his financial interest to mess things up at the shipyard. There's got to be something else."

Louise asked, "Could it be just what it looks like—a bunch of accidents caused by our not knowing what we're doing?"

Opal jumped in, "It could be. Neither Jeannie nor Toots was the most capable out there on the yard. Don't make that face. You know it's true."

Louise wasn't done arguing. "Besides, it's just as likely an inexperienced guy as a gal!"

"Sure, sure," Opal answered. "But also, I don't trust Lowe."

We all stared at her.

"Something's off," she continued. "And I feel like it's coming from him. Don't you think it's strange that he keeps the contest going, even with two women dying and all the accidents and errors piling up? Wouldn't you think he'd cancel everything?"

Sandy answered, "Something weird about a businessman not canceling his moneymaking contests? No, there's nothing strange about it. It's consistent. It's capitalism."

I added, "That's what I'm saying—he's an industrialist. He wouldn't risk his business by bringing attention to people dying on the job."

Belva said, "He obviously likes positive headlines and pictures. It's been a pain to bury all the reports about what's been happening. And they're getting out. That bad publicity hurts him where he lives—the bank account."

I thought, *The hurt isn't just coming from his ledger.*

Opal asked, "What if his drive to kill and control is bigger than his drive for money?"

Twice now. I answered, "That would explain the dead girls. But not the errors piling up. Why the shoddy shipbuilding? Why would he do that?"

"Maybe, since he's such a woman hater, he wants to get out of having women play any role in the shipyard," Opal said.

DEFINITELY PUSHING TOO HARD.

I trained my gaze straight ahead, away from Belva.

Sandy sighed, expressing what the group seemed to feel. We wouldn't know until we knew.

"Don't you have a job for me?" Nancy asked.

"Yes." Jeez, I'd forgotten Nancy, but thought of something fast. "Position yourself midway between Headquarters and Yard Two. Let us know if anything's going wrong while we're in Lowe's office. Just alert us."

"I've got this whistle on my key chain." She held it up.

"That's perfect, Nancy."

"If you hear the whistle, somebody's headed your way."

"Got it."

Sandy said, "So, we've got our plan." Her voice lacked its usual can-do ring, and I felt my confidence dip.

"I'll pay the cashier," I said.

They all put their coins on the table and left. All except Belva.

"So what's part B?" she asked.

I answered her question with one of my own. "Did you think it was weird with Opal?"

"She was pushing Lowe as the bad guy pretty strong. Stronger than I would have expected."

"She's acting even more urgent than usual. Kind of driven," I said.

Belva answered, "So the second part of the plan is . . ."

"To find out about Opal in the files."

"Why'd you let her know we're going in there? Why give her this information?"

"Maybe we'll flush her out."

"Like a hunting dog?"

"Maybe we'll make her nervous enough to leave cover."

———————•———————

CHAPTER THIRTY-EIGHT

DAY SIX

5 P.M., THURSDAY, NOVEMBER 12, 1942

Yard Two
Lowe Shipyard
Richmond, California

Though it had been empty all day, twenty thousand people now crowded onto Yard Two for the night shift and the hoped-for completion of SS *John Wesley Powell*, the beating of Portland's record. Belva and I stood at the edge, trying to catch relevant details within the enormous crowd.

Several swing bands, a barbecue joint, and a bar were assembled under tents just outside the yard, encouraging onlookers and press to gather and report on the finish. It had all been planned by Rupert and his office before Toots died. They must have considered canceling but decided the show must go on. Depressing.

I climbed the first few rungs of a ladder on a fire truck to get a better view. Under spotlights close to the ship's bow, Lowe and Mrs. Pinter stood near a big man I recognized as William Randolph Hearst, a towering gray eminence next to Hedda Hopper in her large red hat. I tasted bile at the sight of them.

I scanned further out and saw Opal at work, alongside other

crew members hustling to finish the ship. I didn't see Louise. She could have been anywhere in the crowd.

I jumped off the ladder and Belva and I walked briskly toward Headquarters, nodding to Nancy and her whistle, standing sentinel on a bench, staring in Lowe's direction. Belva kept looking over her shoulder, but there was no one trailing us, no one anywhere around us. Everybody was where the action was, on Yard Two.

Belva opened Headquarters' front door with her keys and flipped on the light. I flipped it off, giving her a *take no chances* look.

Once in his office, I said, "I'll go through his desk. You do the filing cabinets. You know what we need."

Belva looked worried, though she'd sneaked in here to take things for much less cause. Well, maybe not less cause to her.

"Where are the keys to the cabinets and drawers?" I didn't want to pick every lock.

"Mrs. Pinter keeps them in her top drawer."

I picked that lock, found the ring of little keys, opened all the drawers of Lowe's desk, then gave the keys to Belva.

First, I riffled through the pile on his desktop. It was current correspondence—loan documents, tax stuff, invoices, résumés, covered with scribbles. I tried to read what he'd written in the dim light. Nothing on the desk stood out as important. I noted a fountain pen that matched the one I'd taken from Mrs. Pinter's desk and kept in my pocket.

I started in on his desk drawers, from the bottom up. The lower drawer revealed a heavy folder. I got it out and started reading.

Lowe had tucked the notes about Frank into this folder. Nothing here other than what I already knew. I moved on to the other drawers.

"Here we go," said Belva. I joined her at the cabinet. "Thick folder on women welders—Jeannie, Toots, Nancy, Louise."

"You take two, I'll take two."

We spread them out on the desk, reading as fast as possible.

These were forms they'd filled out, full of names and places and dates. None of it contradicted what we already knew. Toots hadn't given much detail about her parents, not as much as she'd told me, but none of it looked amiss.

I spoke out. "Where's Opal's file? Why isn't hers with the others?"

We had returned to the filing cabinets to hunt when we heard keys jangle outside the main door.

I closed Lowe's drawers and Belva straightened the desk. I retreated to the corner where I'd hid in the dark once before, from Belva herself. She stationed herself against the wall, near Lowe's office door, holding a pile of insignificant files, as if they were the excuse for her being here, alone, in the dark building.

The door opened, and the shrill squealing of Nancy's whistle filled the room. We hadn't heard it behind the closed Headquarters doors, hadn't foreseen danger.

Belva peeked through the crack between the door and its jamb and signaled to me in the direction of Mrs. Pinter's desk. Okay. Belva could manage this. They worked with each other every day.

Mrs. Pinter moved behind her desk, more keys jangling, Belva still watching. I tiptoed to the door behind Belva and, over her head, saw Mrs. Pinter through the crack. She stuffed a number of folders into a bag, locked a desk drawer, and straightened her skirt.

I pinched Belva and she went through the door.

"Hello, Mrs. Pinter."

Mrs. Pinter screeched, "What are you doing here, Belva?"

"What are *you* doing?" Belva asked in a low voice.

Belva walked toward her and they circled each other, until Belva was facing the door I hid behind and Mrs. Pinter's back was to me.

Belva repeated, "I said, what are you doing, Mrs. Pinter?"

"Such a shame, Belva."

Mrs. Pinter reached inside her purse and pulled out a gun and pointed it at Belva. I froze.

"You're too young to understand," Mrs. Pinter said. "I'm sorry. But those of us who believe in an independent American destiny are banding together and organizing for strength. It was a tiny minority of our people that led us into this war. The minority is powerful. It's influential. But it doesn't represent real American people. So people like me will step up to do what's needed. Because we're true patriots."

"True patriots? Sabotaging the war effort?" Belva pushed.

"Getting us out of it! Punishing the politicians who so stupidly got us involved!"

Belva shrieked, "Now!"

I ran straight at Mrs. Pinter, shoving her between the shoulder blades.

She fell to the ground, holding the gun aloft with both hands. She pointed it at me and shot, the recoil sending the gun skittering across the floor.

Belva screamed again, her hands at her mouth. A dark stain spread across the right leg of my pants. The shot must have skimmed me. I felt nothing. Mrs. Pinter scrambled toward her gun and grabbed it before either Belva or I could act.

Now she stood, turned, and pointed the gun again at Belva.

DO IT, JANE! YOU KNOW HOW TO DO THIS!

I ran at Mrs. Pinter a second time, driving the fountain pen from my pocket into the side of Mrs. Pinter's neck, all the way up to my fist. She fell, gagging, to the floor, grasping her wound.

I grabbed her gun, handing it and Mrs. Pinter's bag to Belva.

"Keep the gun on her. Don't take it off! I'm getting to Yard Two."

———o———

DAY SIX

7 P.M., THURSDAY, NOVEMBER 12, 1942

Yard Two
Lowe Shipyard
Richmond, California

I dragged myself, my leg numb, from Headquarters toward Yard Two, every lurching step pulsing shock through my body to my brain, a Morse code directing me to stop.

Nancy met me halfway, gaping at the blood. "Oh my God, Jane!"

"Go help Belva. She's okay, but she's got a gun on Mrs. Pinter. You need to get in there and call the police."

Nancy gulped and ran toward the building. I saw the courage that made her do that, she who wasn't designed for risk. *Oh God, don't let this be one more time . . .*

I couldn't stop and think. I had to keep moving. I stumbled as best I could, so slow, weaker and weaker, with so much blood on my pants, light-headed, everything yellow. I fought the urge to vomit.

Toots had once called Opal a lemming who'd march off a cliff and willingly betray everybody who didn't do things the way she thought was right. Did Toots have a more complete idea about Opal and choose not to tell me?

Opal had taken our bait. I thought there was a chance she'd get in there and remove files herself. I hadn't imagined she'd have Mrs. Pinter try to beat us breaking into Headquarters, trying to get Opal's file before we did. That had to be what was in her drawer. Mrs. Pinter and Opal were partners and they weren't finished, even if Mrs. Pinter was down.

Opal was with Jeannie when she died, electrocuted by a cable Opal must have cut, though she kept claiming it was frayed due to shoddy conditions. She was working at the perfect hour to ruin Nancy's welding in the pipe, to make her and the shipyard look dangerously incompetent. And she was on shift just before Toots fell, staying with her every minute of her photo shoot, even up on the scaffold. Opal must have sabotaged the scaffold and suggested Toots climb it for the picture. She may even have pushed her.

I struggled to move into the dense crowd, everyone I neared looking shocked, no one taking action, just recoiling in horror at my bloody skin and clothes.

The loud, patriotic band was back. Thumping drums, blaring horns, the sound of explosions. Behind them I heard the alarm of sirens, I thought, or maybe that was another band or something in my head.

Two huge cranes lowered another structure on top of the hull and, when it landed, crowds of workers swarmed it like ants on a ham, welding, pounding, attaching, a mass effort of industry.

To the side were Sandy and Hedda, nose to nose, yelling at each other, Hedda's arms waving. Sandy looked angry in a focused sort of way, like a person who wanted to fight. Scheming was one thing. Gratifying, yes. But what she wanted was to erupt, and that's what was happening.

William Randolph Hearst stood to the side, his arms

crossed, smirking at the spectacle of the fighting women. I knew instantly that neither Sandy nor Hedda would benefit from this display in front of a man who at that very moment was putting them each in a box in his head.

NOT LOOKIN' GOOD.

Who cares. You can't lose something you never had.

But where Hearst saw nothing more than a catfight, I saw a woman with power and integrity going to bat for me as she always had. I wasn't going to leave Sandy and the *Prospect* for something Hedda said was better. Better, until something better than me came along. Hedda had Hedda's best interests at heart and always would, not mine, never mine. My future lived at the *Prospect*. I was going to dance with the one that brung me.

WAKE UP. STOP OPAL.

I pulled myself back to the present and craned to search the crowd, trying to see over thousands of helmeted heads. I spotted a scaffold and quaked, thinking of Toots. But I needed the height to stop this. I climbed up one rung and then two. I shivered, maybe from fear, maybe from shock. But I climbed.

My chances of distinguishing anyone in a crowd that size had to be minimal, but somehow Opal stood out. Maybe because that's exactly what she was doing—standing stock-still in the crowd, the only one not moving in a sea of shipyard workers welding, hammering, ferrying steel back and forth. She just stood, her blue plaid shirt glowing in the crowd.

I followed the arrow of her gaze to Louise, moving toward the new section of ship several men were clustered over. Louise grabbed a welding wand sitting on a bench, a wand already attached to its oxygen tank.

I looked back at Opal's intense gaze, full of hate.

I yelled at Louise, "Don't pick it up!"

She couldn't hear me with all that noise, the band, the machinery, the men, and the sirens at Headquarters.

If she loosened the oxygen tank's seal, it would explode. We all would.

I ran for Louise, screaming. She looked up in shock as I tackled her, knocking the wand from her hands, sending Louise into the bay.

Men jumped in the frigid water after her, splashing and yelling.

Lowe grabbed me, pinning my arms.

"What the hell, Jane!" he yelled, seeing the blood all over us both, letting go, his eyes crazed.

Over his shoulder I saw Opal run for the wand. I pushed away Lowe, closing the distance to Opal and tackling her too. She still grasped the wand in her hand but couldn't pull the trigger, stretched out as she was. I pinned her to the deck, smearing her red as I pushed the wand out of her grip.

Around us, trumpets blared, confetti shot out of cannons, crowds roared, sirens whined. The world record had fallen and so had a killer.

———o———

DAY SIX

9 P.M., THURSDAY, NOVEMBER 12, 1942

Field Hospital
Lowe Town
Richmond, California

Anne, the peevish nurse who'd helped me break into the hospital to identify Jeannie, dabbed Betadine as the doctor checked the stitches on my thigh. Mrs. Pinter's bullet had passed right through, taking out a chunk of flesh but not damaging bone or muscle.

"I don't see how you could have gotten much luckier," said the young doctor.

"Thass me, a very lucky ducky."

The doctor glanced at Anne and said, "There's the morphine at work."

Anne smiled at the young doctor and squeezed my shoulder. "You *are* a lucky girl."

There was a knock at the door and an officer peeked in, his face a question mark.

The doctor nodded yes and Belva entered quietly, looking nothing like her usual tidy, just-so self. Her blouse was untucked and her tan skirt bloodstained.

"That my blood or hers?"

"Both, I think."

Anne pulled a chair from the corner of the room up next to my bed for her.

"This one's loopy," the doctor told Belva. "To use a medical term. You can sit here with her for a bit until the police or whoever are ready to interrogate her."

"Tear the gate?" I asked.

Belva asked, "Whoever?"

"I don't know if it will be police or FBI or someone else. They'll want to know what happened. We all do." He was apparently interested in my stabbing a secretary in the neck with a fountain pen.

"How is Mrs. Pinter?" Belva asked.

"No idea," he said.

"Anyway, they'd best ask their questions of Jane after the morphine wears off," Belva said.

"That's what I'll suggest. Let's see if they listen," the doctor said. "Your main job, Jane, is to rest. No risk-taking for a good long while."

"Yessir. Aye aye."

He and Anne left together, her carrying the clipboard.

Belva scooted her chair closer to my bed and leaned down to whisper. "They took Mrs. Pinter off. I don't know where, or if it was the regular police or the military police or FBI."

I struggled to focus. "What did you find out about her?"

"Bits and pieces. No one's sharing much, but I did get some out of Mr. Lowe. You know, when he was kind of susceptible, before he shut off the spigot."

"Suscept . . ." I tried to ask.

"Emotional. Everybody was. It was all so shocking. But he

shared some about Mrs. Pinter before he closed it down. He said it turns out she was a handler, in charge of Opal."

"A handler? Is that a German spy?"

"Not German. She was part of the America First Committee. You know, the isolationists, like Charles Lindbergh and Henry Ford? They thought no foreign power could attack us, and that Nazis defeating Britain wouldn't put us at risk, like that was the only reason to fight."

I thought of my own doubts about getting involved in this war, mainly centering on the fact that I thought it was poor people, like the ones I grew up with, who would do all the fighting and dying. But I sure didn't side with Lindbergh and Ford. I knew crazy when I saw it, though I hadn't seen it in Mrs. Pinter and Opal. Crazy was more subtle than I realized.

Belva went on. "So America First officially broke up after Pearl Harbor. But Mrs. Pinter was part of a splinter group, trying to sabotage the war effort. Sounds like the leftovers were largely racist. I guess they hate Jewish people." She looked shaken.

"So she was trying to sabotage the liberty ship program?"

"The push to hire women workers was harmful to their goal of getting out of the fight."

"She wasn't doing this planning on her own, was she? She doesn't seem like the type." I was struggling with the gap between what she seemed and what she was, something I should have been more aware of, given my own history of faking my identity.

"How would we know what a spy type is? Lowe was upset about that too, asked me if I had any idea. I didn't. He said handlers like her are hard to spot because their job requires them to be unobtrusive. They're usually middle-aged with nothing special about them, except maybe with more money than they really should have."

The morphine was wearing off, and I could picture Mrs. Pinter, the first time I saw her, in a peach wool suit with an ugly brooch on her lapel. Then another time in that blue suit. And another in green. Every time I saw her, she had a new suit, made of thick, quality fabric. Her clothes were nothing I'd want, but I recognized they were of quality, maybe more expensive than what a normal secretary could afford.

"She was dressed dowdy, but expensive."

"There you go."

"What about Opal?" I asked.

"Mr. Lowe says Mrs. Pinter turned her."

"Turned?"

"Recruited her."

I expected Opal would like being recruited. But I couldn't make sense of the rest of it.

"Why? And where is Opal now?"

"No idea."

"Would you do me a favor? Find out?"

"Sure." Belva squeezed my hand before she got up to leave. "One more thing. Mickey says you were right—the acetylene tank was unscrewed. It would have blown us all into the water."

It was a relief to get something right. My head was blurry and there was so much to disturb me, but the thing that did most of all was that I hadn't accurately seen the danger. I went straight to suspecting Lowe because of what I'd assumed about his romantic history and then Mickey because he just seemed like a general woman hater. Even when there were clues in front of me, I didn't process that the danger came from a plump, aging secretary and a finicky, A+ critic. I needed to think about why I thought the way I did.

CHAPTER FORTY-ONE

DAY SIX

10 P.M., THURSDAY, NOVEMBER 12, 1942

Field Hospital
Lowe Town
Richmond, California

Belva rolled me down the antiseptic-smelling hall in a wheelchair, a blanket over my lap. A few of what looked like plainclothes officers circled off to the side near the nurses' station, whispering to each other, arguing quietly, just enough hullabaloo to prevent them from noticing us.

Belva jerked her head at a door. I nodded and she opened it quietly.

Opal lay in bed, handcuffed to a metal rail. Her cheek was torn up, which made me think of the way I'd tackled her, her face hitting the deck.

Belva closed the door behind us and rolled me up close to Opal.

"Have you come to throw me out the window or something?"

"As if you weren't the only cold-blooded killer in the room."

"That's not what this was," she said, irritated.

"Really? Is Jeannie dead? Is Toots? Were you just this afternoon trying to kill everybody down on the dock, blow up all of us?" I could feel something rising in me, some combination of anger and morphine.

"It's a question of mathematics."

"Oh, sure, it's math."

"A handful of deaths that might prevent a lot more. I don't want *anybody* to die, nobody! I want to stop all this ridiculous fighting, the waste of life and money and resources, and this was how to do it." Who was she trying to convince?

"That's the stupidest thing I've ever heard. You just hate Jewish people, don't you? Like the America Firsters. That's what this is!" I answered, furious.

"That is not me. That's the opposite of me. Do you have any idea why I took part in this operation?" Spit flew as she yelled.

"No, I couldn't possibly know why you'd do something so heartless." I should have calmed myself down, to listen better, but I was just so angry.

"Heartless? You don't know me." She clutched at the fabric of the hospital gown over her heart. "I grew up on a farm. We take *care* of things and people. I had a fiancé, Paul." She choked back a sob. "A beautiful, decent boy, the *most* decent boy, from the farm next to ours. He was a Tanaka. He had taken charge of their farm, learned it all from his father and grandfather. They had big plans, for walnuts." She wept into her unshackled hand before continuing. "Then, after Pearl Harbor, he started to pre-pare the farm so his younger siblings and father could manage it so he could enlist, to fight the Germans and Japanese, even though his parents came from Japan! He was so patriotic toward this country, he would fight his cousins if he had to. My father was going to help the Tanakas out too. Everybody supported Paul's enlisting."

I had a terrible feeling.

"Just two months later, FDR and the governor took away the whole Tanaka family, all of them, even the grade school children, took them to a relocation center. Paul and I were going to be married! I was going to marry the best man I'd ever met, and the government threw him in prison because of this war. And they didn't do it because of anything he'd done wrong. They did it just because of who he was."

I looked at Belva, whose face was troubled, confused, probably mirroring my own.

I said, "They'll let him out." I knew this was weak, that it didn't help.

Opal laughed bitterly. "They were sent to a holding station, Walerga Park, just outside of Sacramento, supposedly until the government could build enough camps to keep them all. With the temporary buildings so close together there, no proper sanitation, five thousand people. No vaccines." Tears wet her face like rain on a sheer granite peak. "Paul contracted polio."

I didn't say anything. I couldn't breathe. I thought of the many people I knew who'd contracted polio, the leg braces, the iron lung, the isolation, the pain.

"Paul died in that prison. And I died too."

Now my own lungs emptied. Nothing could have helped Opal after this. "You blame the government."

"Obviously! And don't give me some platitude about how we're helping fight racism over there, against the Germans. We're not fighting racism. We're locking people up because of their race right here in this country, people like Paul. Just ask her!" She stretched her long left arm out, pointing it at Belva. "Ask her if we're fighting racism."

Belva got taller in her body.

"Don't you speak to me," Belva said. "Don't pull me into

this, trying to justify what you've done, acting like it's about your sense of justice. It's not. You lost your lover and you're mad. I get that. But don't connect it to me. I've been a victim plenty of times, but you don't see me killing anybody."

The police officers burst into the room in a gang, shocked to find us there. "Who are you?" they chorused. "You can't be here!" "Nurse!"

There was so much commotion, nurses and more police. I sat, tensed in my wheelchair, trapped by injury, unclear what was actually happening.

Opal's back and neck arched, her eyes rolled up, foam bubbled out her lips, onto her chin.

A doctor yelled, "In her mouth!"

They swarmed her, trying to pry open her jaw, reach in and take what had set her off. She bit and chomped the hands of the people aiming to save her. She seemed conscious through all of it, staring at me, her eyes widely round, daring me to watch what was happening to her, what she was doing to herself, because now I knew why she was doing it.

Then it was over. The thrashing only lasted a minute before she slumped into her mattress. The police and medical crew breathed hard from the exertion and stress. An older doctor reached into her mouth and pulled out a glass cyanide capsule in the shape of her molar.

CHAPTER FORTY-TWO

DAY SEVEN

9 A.M., FRIDAY, NOVEMBER 13, 1942

Headquarters
Lowe Town
Richmond, California

I sat across the mahogany desk from Lowe. He looked different now, weathered, aging years in a week. In place of his usual suit he wore a misshapen Irish fisherman's sweater, like he didn't care what people thought about him. I saw that it made him more appealing, an advantage powerful men had, the ability to grow more attractive, not less, with time and trouble.

Rupert sat stiffly to my right, which was a little awkward after our night of drinking at Jiggs and what came afterward, though in the wake of everything else, I wrote that off as an unsavory work event. Another choice not to be repeated.

Sandy sat to my left, prim posture, pressed suit, tidy hair, pretty as always, but no Sandy smile. I wondered at their pulling her rather than Edward in for this meeting. Maybe her gamble, pretending she had more power than she did, had worked. Or maybe they recognized she was the one at the *Prospect* with her hands all over the whole poster girl thing. Officially, maybe more than I did.

Somebody I didn't know, some kind of soldier, stood like a totem in the back of the room.

WHY'S HE HERE?

Lowe began, sounding raspy and sour. "I cannot sufficiently impress upon you how important it is that you neither speak nor write anything about this episode." His voice had a lot of smoke and drink in it this morning.

He was trying to avoid the bad PR. I could work with that. I said, "We foiled their plan, we stopped them. That's the story." In spite of my bone-deep desolation about Jeannie and Toots, still I wanted to persuade him. It was hard to stop being myself, valuing what I valued.

Rupert hissed. We were no longer on the same team.

"Thank you for that, Jane," Lowe said. "For stopping them at the finish line. That's the main thing." He seemed sincere enough. "But . . . not before they slowed production and killed two people." He paused, gathering himself before continuing. "Not to mention infiltrating our shipbuilding program completely. Who knows what they've shared with the enemy. We cannot let that get out when we're trying to *build* morale, not dismantle it, in order to save lives."

"Doesn't it seem like this could help, like all the posters say —*loose lips sink ships*? We should let everybody know there are spies all around us. And we can catch them by paying attention."

"Loose lips, exactly," Rupert said, pointing at me. "*This* will not be the larger narrative."

"I'm a journalist, Rupert!"

"Really, Jane?"

"Rupert," Sandy interrupted.

I had a lot of latitude in my columns about what to cover, what to leave out. It was mainly my choice about what interested me, up to a point. At this moment, Sandy Zimmer was that point. She didn't look entirely up to it, her face wan, her eyes red. She was off. But Sandy was my team. She spoke up.

"You did a great, heroic thing, Jane. That's the truth."

I felt the bad news coming. She hadn't said *though* or *although*, but I could feel it underneath the sentence. Had she been working with Lowe on this response?

"Jane, we aren't running this story," Sandy finished.

"Don't you care about newsworthiness? We have to share what we know."

"I understand, Jane. As you clearly know. But this is wartime. I care more about our country."

Where was this coming from? Was this some kind of act? We'd uncovered the work of traitors, and we weren't going to shout it from the rooftops? "Are you saying you don't think a reporter ought to be free to report the truth in this country?"

Her face shifted, much more stressed than she'd seemed a week ago. "Grow up, Jane. Everything's relative. Everything depends on everything else."

This was the message I always got. *You're too immature to understand. It's more complicated than you understand.* But that wasn't true. I didn't fail to understand the complexity. It was just that I disagreed with the conclusion. Newspapers tell what they find.

Sandy went on. "I know this is a loss. But we can make it up to you."

"Oh, really?" I was hot as a torch. I didn't care about anything but revealing what had happened. It was significant and needed to be told.

The phone rang and Lowe picked it up, listened, then said, "Give us a minute," and hung up.

Sandy continued, "I understand your doing what you did means you spoiled a chance to jump ship." My cheeks went hot. "Hedda told me about the offer she dangled, and that you said yes."

"Sandy, I didn't—"

"I can see why Hearst would have been a serious step up for you. Definitely. And he's more than willing to publish whatever sells. The *Prospect* can't give you what Hearst could. We're just a small group of papers." She looked directly at me, only at me, straight-faced, a businessperson. "But we'll syndicate you. And we'll double your salary, pay you what a man would earn."

In spite of my basement-low spirits, I felt that have its effect. "Why don't I do that research on what a guy would earn?" I said.

"Don't push your luck, Jane."

"I'm not happy. This is all just wrong, journalistically—"

"Please. Count your blessings, Jane."

I didn't argue now, just tried to figure it out. "Does Zimmer understand this arrangement you're making?" I didn't want to undercut her authority, but I wanted to understand this step up, syndication and more money.

Lowe looked out the window. Sandy said, "It's taken care of."

WHAT'S GOING ON HERE?

"Go ahead and bring him in, please," Lowe said to the soldier in the back of the room.

There was some uneasy shuffling, and then Lowe, Rupert, and Sandy all stood. I turned and saw a man in uniform enter the room.

"General," said Lowe.

The rest of them nodded soberly.

He looked straight at me. "Miss Benjamin," he said.

I belatedly stood, confused.

"I'm Jimmy Doolittle."

I took his offered hand, holding my breath.

"I understand you're from Sacramento. I spent some time there, at the McClellan Air Base. Nice town, Sacramento." Doolittle had kind eyes.

"Thank you." What else could I say?

"I've been to see Tommie, and she told me I need to talk to you too."

"Sir . . ."

He cleared his throat. "I'm not sure how much you know about Frank O'Rourke's status."

I looked at Lowe, who said, "Rupert, Sandy, everybody else out of the room."

They moved to exit.

When the door closed behind them, Lowe said, "General, I've told her about Vladivostok."

Doolittle nodded, took a few quiet steps toward the window, and then turned to face me again. "Here's what else I can share. Frank has been remarkably brave. We're making plans to bring him and the other fellas home."

My face went wet with relief, as if so much worry had dammed up behind my eyes.

He continued, "But it's complicated. We're talking to the Russians. We hadn't finalized an arrangement before Frank's plane landed there. That's why the actual plan was to make it to China. The Russians are sensitive to the Japanese response. They don't want to simply return our boys and upset Japan. We're arranging a way they can escape."

"You're negotiating with the Russians?"

"As I said, it's complicated. It takes time. But we're working on it. I just want you to know, I haven't given up on Frank. He didn't give up on the rest of us."

That made a knot in my chest pulse like a living thing. As resentful as I'd been at Frank for leaving me with Tommie's needs to tend, I saw now I was mostly envious that he had the opportunity to be brave in such a significant way, as I'd like to be.

General Doolittle rose and said, "Thank you for everything you've done, Jane. Lowe told me about the past week. You've made a real contribution here. We'll never be able to measure the difference you've made."

Then he shook my hand again and left Lowe and me alone in the room.

Lowe said, "I'm going to make sure Frank gets home. Now you make sure to stay quiet."

What I had to report was significant. But it could do harm.

Lowe went on, "You should understand the importance of discretion more than most."

"Why do you say that?"

"Because you have secrets."

"Who've you been talking to?"

"I'm not saying."

HE KNOWS ABOUT YOU AND INEZ. SHE BETRAYED YOU.

He continued, "Secrets can be powerful when they're kept and destructive when they aren't."

OR IT'S HEDDA, TRYING TO WORK LOWE AGAINST YOU.

I rose to leave.

Lowe stopped me. "You asked me before what had changed, what I thought before and what I think now."

I waited.

"At first I didn't think Jeannie had been killed. I thought I'd put her in a job she wasn't equipped for. I doubted her skill. Because she was so . . . lovely, I doubted her competence. I hate that I doubted her." His jaws clenched.

I had similar regrets.

"Also, I don't think you've heard. Edward Zimmer had a heart attack. He passed away this morning."

No. I looked at the door Sandy had passed through. Was she still there? Already gone? I looked back at Lowe.

"What was Sandy doing here?"

"She knew she needed to be here for you. You ought to be there for her. Go on," he said.

I ran from his office, past Mrs. Pinter's desk to the road, where I saw Sandy's driver turning right toward the exit, back to San Francisco.

Sandy lost her husband, and yet still showed up for me. She always showed up.

I dropped to the curb, put my head in my hands, and cried.

CHAPTER FORTY-THREE

DAY SEVEN

11 A.M., FRIDAY, NOVEMBER 13, 1942

OWI Quonset
Lowe Town
Richmond, California

I sat at the long metal desk alone. Everybody else had packed up and gone back to their newsrooms. I didn't know exactly what to do, just that I had to finish this. For all my many faults, still, I cared about doing my job. I could not leave one more unhappy chapter of my life unfinished. I cared.

I started typing unscripted thoughts, beginning with the words *Our Poster Girl.* I thought a poster girl ought to represent the very essence of an idea.

I knew Toots hadn't ever really been a poster girl for women welders at this shipyard. She was wonderful, funny, warm, smart, adventuresome. I would have wanted to be her friend forever. But she was not our poster girl. Yet I pushed her so hard to do it, because it was better for me to resolve it, and she was the straightest path left. But it was never right and it led to her death.

Opal was a poster girl for something else, maybe for the idea that grief and injustice can ruin a person and we shouldn't be surprised when it does. Some of us build rugged scar tissue over our injuries and just keep going. For others, the scar itself creates the condition that kills us. There was almost no way to know in advance which way it would work for a person. But I knew it wasn't about merit.

I hadn't changed my mind about Louise. I knew that if her abortion came out, it would ruin her and ruin the good any poster campaign might do for the cause, even if I disliked the way I had taken that decision from Louise herself.

Was Nancy our girl? Sweet, pretty, kind Nancy?

I started typing, to give it a go, trying to dredge up the nerve-charged energy to make this claim.

A shadow crossed my page. I looked over my shoulder to find Rupert reading.

"You think you should just go ahead and do this, after everything?" he asked.

I was too tired to fight. "Rupert, I'm not writing what happened. I'll leave that to the others. It's not my role. I get it. Somebody's going to tell the truth, but it won't be me. Just let me finish out this gig and go back to work."

"You're an idiot," he said. He dropped a copy of the *Los Angeles Times* on my desk, folded open to Hedda's column.

HEDDA HOPPER'S HOLLYWOOD
November 13, 1942

Pretty Rosie Parker is as easy to look at as overtime pay on your weekly check. And she's a good example of the old contention that glamour isn't about the clothes but what goes into the clothes.

Prewar fashion frills make silly wartime clothing for women. Rosie wears heavy shoes, a dark suit, and a turban to keep her hair out of

harm's way. And the harm she's avoiding? The
machinery she works on at the Alameda Naval Air
Station.

Rosie is a riveter. She learned how to do it so
she could play her role, building the airplanes
that will win this war. I met Rosie while
cheering Bay Area workers who do their part to
save our boys on the front lines.

Rosie is smart and patriotic and pretty as you
please.

She's Rosie the Riveter.

Could you be a Rosie? I say, "You can do it!"

Sick to my stomach, I stopped reading and looked at the
picture alongside the column. Rosie was a tall, thin beauty, with
her dark hair swathed in a polka dot bandana, a jumpsuit with
wide shoulders and a very narrow waist. She was absolutely
adorable—a perfect poster girl.

"She's torpedoed Wendy the Welder."

"Her name's not even Rosie, of course," Rupert said.

"She did what we were going to," I added.

"Who knows how many falsehoods are in here. But Hedda
beat us to it," he said.

Yes, she did.

I couldn't tell if I even cared. I didn't want the Wendy the
Welder thing, not in the way I'd originally planned it. That
wasn't good enough anymore, and I'd known it even before I saw
how it looked when Hedda stole it out from under me.

Sure, Rosie the Riveter was going to do some good. But not
enough.

I ripped the paper out of the typewriter, wadded it up, and tossed it in the can.

"It doesn't matter," I said.

"Not any of it?"

"Well," I said, "I don't like Hedda double-crossing me." I thought of the fake offer of the Hearst position. She'd been stalling me.

"I'm not entirely sure this was a double-cross, officially, but frankly the language of espionage and warcraft eludes me. I think you were double-crossing her too, so do those two things cancel each other out?"

"Maybe. I don't know."

Rupert shrugged and wandered off. He was probably right about my less-than-sterling tactics. But still I was frightened to think that Hedda might have been investigating my abortion. I knew that news could ruin me and it made me furious, not just that Hedda could possibly do this but that my abortion had that power over my future.

And it wasn't clear what I could do about any of it.

CHAPTER FORTY-FOUR

DAY SEVEN

NOON, FRIDAY, NOVEMBER 13, 1942
The Prospect Building
San Franciso, California

I was never any good at expressing sympathy. I hadn't been trained right in how to say the needed thing, and I sure didn't have any good examples from my parents. That often kept me from trying. But this time couldn't be like that.

I walked through the *Prospect* newsroom. My colleagues were all somber. The war had whacked the fun out of the floor for the past year, as we were all aware on a daily basis of the very real trouble in the world. And today was worse. Nobody knew what would happen.

Today Congress had approved the drafting of men eighteen and nineteen years old. That hit home as I passed Wally, Barry, Quentin, and Shawn, reporters I'd come up with on the copy-boy bench when they were mostly eighteen and nineteen. Now they were spread among assignments to the City Desk, War News, Sports, Business. I looked at them now, and it was hard to believe how naive we all were five years ago. And that those boys would have been headed to war today. The war had been with us for a while. But today, the trouble seemed very personal.

The guys nodded and smiled tightly at me, dipping their heads, as I passed.

Looking directly at Wally, I pointed at Zimmer's office, a question in my eyes. He nodded.

I knocked at the corner office door, heard a faint "Yes?" and entered.

Sandy sat at Zimmer's desk, buried in the next day's pages and surrounded by front page mock-ups, legal pads, and charts on the wall.

She looked so small against Zimmer's desk and chair. Too small.

Words congealed in my throat. I couldn't do this. But then I didn't have to.

Sandy ran around the desk and threw her arms around my neck. The dam burst, for both of us. We cried and held on to each other for dear life through our tears. I found the way to comfort her, by not presuming to know what to do. Just being there, not talking, holding her.

Finally, she let go.

She was grieving, but she was still Sandy, in her well-fitted black dress, her tidy hair, and no jewelry other than her wedding ring.

"Jehoshaphat," she said, which qualified as swearing for Sandy.

I didn't know if I should speak at all, but I went ahead anyway. "Did you have any idea this was happening to him?"

"No. I was just mad, thrown off, by his irritability. I knew something was wrong, of course. He wasn't acting the way he usually did toward me."

She looked at me very pointedly.

"You may not know this, or may assume it was otherwise,

but Edward was very respectful toward me. I know you think he should have given me more responsibility, but he encouraged me to come in here every day and to make decisions by his side, and to make plenty of them on my own too."

I had focused on her not having the title or the pay she deserved. But she did have the work and the influence. I saw that now. I regretted how dismissive I'd been of Zimmer, how willing I'd been to cast him in my own narrow view of what I thought he was, instead of seeing the broader picture in front of me. I guess that's what happens. You rethink what you originally thought. The trick is to learn to do it before people die and it's too late to adjust.

At least Zimmer had done for Sandy what no one would now ever have the chance to do for Jeannie, Toots, or Opal. But I could try to do it for others.

"What's going to happen to the paper?" I asked timidly.

Sandy took my hands in hers.

"Jane, he put it in his will. I'm the publisher."

"Wait. You're the publisher of the *San Francisco Prospect*?"

"No, you're not hearing me. I'm the publisher of the Zimmer Consortium of Newspapers."

"All? All of them?"

"All of them."

I thought I might faint. Sandy was the publisher.

"But what will you . . . How will you . . . How will it work?" I stammered.

"I don't know yet. After the funeral, I'll meet with the lawyers and the money people and then with the managing editors. There's a lot to figure out."

"I am so touched and overwhelmed," I said. "As much for you getting the opportunity you deserve and are qualified for—"

"Well, partly qualified for. Maybe as much as any other publisher who inherits a newspaper group through family connection." She laughed at herself.

"I am just bowled over and inspired."

"Don't be, Jane."

"What?"

"I'm inspired by *you*. I married my way into this. You know I did. I used my wiles, you know that too, to get Edward to marry me. Then along the way we fell in love and became terrific partners and friends. But everything you've achieved has been because of your work and your nerve and your Jane-ness."

Now we were both snotty messes. I regressed and wiped my nose on my sleeve. You can take a girl out of Hooverville, but you can't take Hooverville out of a girl. Sandy laughed.

I said, "That's not true, Sandy. Your kindness to me. Your taking care of me. It meant everything. It made the difference. I couldn't do anything without you."

"That's how it works. We take care of each other."

"But I did consider jumping to Hearst." I lapsed into racking sobs. How close I'd come to ruining all I'd accomplished, for both myself and my best friend. The guilt and humiliation tasted awful in my mouth.

"You're ambitious, Jane. You *should* be ambitious. And because I heard about it, you're getting what you deserve. It's right. It's all right."

She handed me a clean handkerchief, folded on her desktop, and took a second one for herself. Leave it to Sandy to have a collection of clean folded handkerchiefs when they were most needed.

She went on. "I'm going to take my time about getting started. Not too much time, but I'm going to do right by Edward with the funeral service and all that before going full bore here. But first, what are we going to do about Hedda?"

Even now, how quickly she could jump from task to task.

"I've been thinking about that," I admitted.

"She bamboozled you. She likely didn't even talk to Hearst."

"Probably not. But it's strange, especially since you've just agreed to syndicate me—and I don't want you to back out—but I don't want to be like Hedda. I don't want to be a junior Queen Mean, some Princess of Pain or something."

Sandy laughed, the lines at her eyes warming me. It felt good to laugh while crying.

"I want to do it different, Sandy."

"I'm listening."

"I don't want to be a gossip columnist like Hedda or Louella. I want to be funny, yes, quirky, sometimes poking the people on top who lord it over the rest of us. But I want to write a column that tells what a gorgeous, stupid, brilliant, infuriating town and world this is. I want it to be a pop song and guidebook and gossip sheet and a laugh riot. I want it to tell the truth about living here."

"I don't think I'm familiar with something like that."

"Everybody's going to love it. Not just the women. Everybody."

"Everybody?" One end of her mouth ticked up, but she said, "We'll give it a try."

"Except the first new column. That one may be a little different."

The door opened, and a secretary I'd never met leaned into the room. "Mrs. Zimmer, Leo from the union is here. He's asking for the publisher."

Sandy looked at me. "He probably thinks it's a good strategy to come now, figuring I'm in no position to push back."

I laughed. "He's got a lesson coming."

She looked at her watch. "Am I going to be okay with the column?"

I owed this woman everything. It was long past time to start paying it back.

"You will," I promised. And I meant it.

CHAPTER FORTY-FIVE

DAY SEVEN

7 P.M., FRIDAY, NOVEMBER 13, 1942

274 Guerrero, Mission District
San Francisco, California

A new butler answered Mrs. Burns's doorbell this time, slighter and friendlier than the last.

"Miss Benjamin, am I correct?"

The hair on my neck raised with apprehension.

"From the *Prospect*? Oh my, I just love your column! You're very funny!"

"Why, thank you. What's your name, may I ask?"

"Mr. Gibbett," he said, with some dignity. "F. Gibbett. Like my father before me."

F. Gibbett. Flibberti Gibbett. My first thought was, this man had to go in my column. But then I thought, No, I wouldn't put Mrs. Burns's household in the news, no matter how tempting. Even for a terrific butler name.

"Do come in. I know you and Mrs. Burns are friends. She mentioned you just today. There's a party, you know."

"I figured. It *is* Friday night."

I followed him into the big parlor, where all kinds of drinkers and talkers and laughers mingled noisily. From the looks of their glasses, Mrs. Burns was still managing to procure bottles of the real stuff, not just champagne but distilled drinks too. Nobody was drinking soldier beer at this party. At the end of the room, a crooner sang "Tangerine," backed by a tuxedoed band. Life was normal at Mrs. Burns's house.

She came rushing to me with a hug.

"I'm sorry about everything, Jane. It's heartbreaking. Truly."

"Thank you, Mrs. Burns. Please pardon my abruptness, but do you mind if we go over there for a little privacy?" I pointed to a dark empty corner of the room and started walking before she had the chance to object. She followed, shooing away a waiter who rushed to offer cocktails.

I jumped in. "I may be at risk. I know we're all at risk. But I've been hearing things—"

"A little birdie, isn't that what you say?"

"Yes, a few little birdies, one of which is you, have whispered that somebody is snooping around, talking about the possibility of my having been your patient. I need to know how seriously to take this."

She frowned. "You know I don't talk to people who ask such questions."

"I understand. But you know who's snooping. I'm figuring it's Hedda Hopper. She's got knives out for me, and obviously this information would be pretty useful for her. I need to know if she's coming for me to make it public. Or if this is a thing she's going to use in other ways."

"I see." Mrs. Burns folded her arms across her stomach and tilted up her chin, thinking. "I can imagine it would be reasonable to think Hedda Hopper is snooping about you in this way, but she has not asked me."

That threw me. "Then who is it?"

Mrs. Burns closed her mouth and stood, silent.

She would never talk. Was the answer in this room?

Standing next to Mrs. Burns, I scanned the party. A circle of politicos, ladies on their arms. The police chief and his deputy, their heads together. Trios of beautiful women sprinkled throughout, tittering, nervously looking for men to land. Then I saw a large circle of noisy people, a couple of them singing disruptively. At their center stood Tommie, laughing, a cigarette in one hand, champagne in the other, her golden charm drawing the others to her.

I stared until I caught her eye. She smiled. Then she looked at Mrs. Burns at my side, and her smile froze.

I strode across the room to the splashiest person at the party.

"Excuse me, boys," Tommie said, coy even in an emergency.

We walked a few steps away.

"Yes, Jane?"

"Why did you do it?"

She didn't bother denying it. "Because I wanted to know what went on between you and Frank. You're terribly strange about him, and me too, frankly. I've suspected for a long time. If it makes you feel better, Inez didn't tell me."

That did make me feel better. Then I felt worse again because somebody else had told her. For once, I waited without speaking.

Tommie blew a smoke ring and watched it dissipate over my head. "It was your mother."

SOUNDS ABOUT RIGHT.

"It's not her fault," Tommie insisted. "I tricked her."

I disagreed. "You didn't trick Momma. She never does anything she doesn't intend to do."

"I did trick her. I saw her at the roadhouse. I followed her to the bathroom. I made sure nobody else was in there, and I said,

'You know, I think Jane is still disturbed by her procedure at Inez's.'"

I gasped inwardly at her nerve but remained silent.

"Then your momma just laughed, I mean she laughed hard. And she said, 'Don't be stupid. She's over it. She was over it the minute it was done.'"

But Momma was wrong. I wasn't *over it*.

I would always be at risk, because the person who probably loved me more than anyone else in the world, sad as I was to admit it, could not keep her mouth shut about me. She knew information was power, and she craved power, more than anything else, even when she'd prefer not to crave it.

I thought of Louise, and all the many other women like us, and wondered if we would, always and forever, be unsafe like this, captive to this secret.

"You asked Lowe too?"

Now she colored up. "I'm sorry. I shouldn't have. I asked him when he told me about Frank. But he didn't talk."

"What are you planning to do with this secret?"

"Nothing," she said.

"Even when Frank comes home?"

Her eyes misted. "Do you think he'll come home?"

For all Tommie's glamour and fame, she was still so dependent on others, and didn't seem to have any initiative or creativity in her without someone loyal at her side, at least not lately. I felt empathy drip through my veins and decided to think about Frank and Tommie right now, instead of myself.

"He'll come home, Tommie. He'll come home a hero."

——————•——————

CHAPTER FORTY-SIX

DAY SEVEN

10 P.M., FRIDAY, NOVEMBER 13, 1942

Yard Three
Lowe Shipyard
Richmond, California

Belva and I sat on the dock, our feet dangling again over the bay in the undeveloped Yard Three, where I'd asked her to meet me. The wind blew off the water like always. The big flags still flew over Yard Two. The contest was over, but there was a new ship to build. We could hear the thumping and machines, but now that seemed almost like the invisible noise of typewriters to me. Almost comforting, the background sound of work, of progress.

It had only been one week since I got here, and so much had changed.

"I want to say thank you," I said.

"For what?" Belva asked, leaning back on her hands.

"You were always aware of what was wrong. From the beginning." I thought of her whispering to Lowe the first time I saw her, delivering the news he had to hear, willing to be the one who said it.

She shook her head, disturbed. "If I'd been really aware, then Toots wouldn't have died. I didn't figure that out."

"You had a better sense of it than I did. Sometimes I wonder about my instincts."

Belva said, "That's the thing, I guess. Instinct can be wrong, even when it feels one hundred percent right."

"Do you know what Doolittle's famous for?" I'd done some reading up, to know whose hands Frank's life depended on.

"More than the raid?" she asked.

"Related to it. His research specialty was how a pilot has to learn to trust his instruments, not just his senses, because what he sees and feels can be unreliable if he doesn't test them against his instruments."

"How's that work?"

"He taught Frank and the other pilots to forget looking out the windows of their planes, to rely on their cockpit systems, because they were a more accurate extension of their mind. That's supposed to be how they did that raid." I tried to picture choosing not to stare out the window of a plane I was flying.

"I don't know. Frank's plane went down," she said.

"True. Seems like you should do both. Trust your instinct, but test it against the evidence. Seems like you should use every tool you've got." I needed to remember that.

"Use what you've got," she echoed.

I said, "Belva, I'm going to make you the poster girl."

She groaned. "No, are you crazy? I don't even weld here."

"Not yet."

"Don't be stupid, Jane."

"They told me what I can't say. I can't do a poster campaign exactly, but I can do what's right. Everybody says you're the best. Even Opal said it."

"Well, I am the best," Belva agreed, laughing.

"You know what else Opal said? 'Nothing happens if nobody pushes.'"

She returned, "Opal was a killer and a spy."

"And she was in love with someone who'd been terribly wronged. By his own country."

Neither of us spoke for a moment. Belva knew something about that situation.

"Okay," she said. "But you understand nothing's going to happen if you make a poster of me, don't you? The shipyard isn't going to push Wendy the Welder if I'm Wendy. They're not going to let Negro girls weld."

"No, they won't right away. Anyhow, now that there's Rosie the Riveter, it scarcely matters. There won't be room for a Wendy poster campaign. But I can do *something*. I won't regret trying. I'm going to put you in my column with a picture. Some people will read it. It'll make a little difference, I bet. What use is a column if I can't even do that?"

"Should you at least have a contest or something, with whatever new girls get their union cards, to see who's the best?"

"No need. Total waste of time."

"Why?"

"I already know. I've known for a while, Belva. You're the one."

She went silent for a bit. I held my tongue and my breath.

I pulled the folded column out of my pocket and extended it to her. "I'd like you to read it."

"And if I don't like what you've done . . ."

"I won't use it." I passed her the typed copy and she read it, sitting there beside me on the dock, wind whipping the paper in her hands.

BETWEEN TWO BRIDGES, by Jane Benjamin
Saturday, November 14, 1942

We live in trying times. Sometimes it feels like the world is spinning off its axis, about to change its very nature. The best of us are not as good as we should be. The worst are more villainous than ever.

And yet most of us long to help, to protect those who need our help. And most of us agree we should support that effort, make it easy to help.

That's why Adam Lowe, owner of Lowe Shipyard, is paving the way for women to help win this war, in spite of the resentment and backlash he and these women receive for their work building American liberty ships. Progress advances with every woman who gets herself trained and signs on for duty in a shipyard or aircraft plant.

We celebrate the women who do their duty. Huzzah, Rosie the Riveter! But it isn't possible for all of us to become a Rosie. We don't all stand on equal ground.

Consider one such woman, Belva Sanders, who works as a respected clerk for Adam Lowe himself. She does solid, reliable work in that role.

Yet Miss Sanders is an experienced welder. Only twenty-one now, she has apprenticed as a welder since she was seventeen. Her Oakland family home is surrounded by her handiwork—fences, gates, trellises, benches, even tools for managing the cattle that graze alongside their home. Miss Sanders has developed exceptional skill at her trade.

She would clearly be a useful addition to the welding corps at any shipyard. But Miss Sanders is not allowed to do this work because she does not have her Boilermakers Union card.

Because she is Negro.

Because of the color of her skin, Miss Sanders is relegated to auxiliary union membership, which only allows her to work at shipyard jobs with lower pay, where her skills can't be fully applied, where she can't do as much as she's capable of to aid the war effort.

That seems terrifically stupid. Don't you agree?

Imagine what we lose by not allowing all the Belvas to take their rightful place among us, by not letting them do the work we need because downtown San Francisco union men are too afraid to share what they now hoard for themselves.

Yet the world is ready for change. And there's no better place to begin it than right here, right now, in The City That Knows How.

When she'd finished, Belva stood and I did too.

She extended her hand and said, "Deal."

I reached out, gripped her warm hand, and felt a current run through my fingers, up my arm, into my torso, to the top of my stinging scalp, and all the way down to my curling toes. Utterly electrified, the muscles of my fingers contracted so that I couldn't let go, increasing the severity of my reaction. I swore I could feel my muscles, ligaments, and tendons tearing, my flesh burning, my heart being shocked into a total disorder of its usual rhythm. I felt as if I'd lost consciousness for long minutes, though when I was finally able to release her hand, Belva's face didn't look horrified as I expected. She smiled, like all this was normal. Blood pulsed in my ears, but Belva didn't seem to hear it.

I didn't know what this incident signified, other than that I was changed. It would take decades to see the many ways in which that would prove true.

Though Ben figured it out faster than I did.

SO YOU GOT A WORKING HEART AFTER ALL, SISTER.

Author's Note

My husband, Andy, loves World War II movies. We watch a lot of them. Usually, it begins by him saying, "Seems like a World War II night." I generally answer, "Okay. Let's watch one with women in it." That's a harder challenge than you might think. It led us to the Rosie the Riveter World War II Home Front Museum on the waterfront in Richmond, California, a visit that inspired much of *Poster Girl*.

In this book, as in the others in the Jane Benjamin series, fictional characters, incidents, and settings are based on real historical figures, events, and places. In every case, I modified historical elements to fit the needs of historical mystery fiction. Any dastardly deed committed by one of my characters is entirely invented.

Adam Lowe, a character who first appears in *Tomboy*, is inspired by the industrialist achievements of Henry J. Kaiser, who won a number of contracts with the US Maritime Commission to build flexible and inexpensive cargo ships—liberty ships—during the 1930s. Then, in 1940, he was awarded a large contract with the British government for sixty liberty ships to replace what the Germans had sunk in the Battle of Britain. Kaiser built his shipyard in the Richmond area in 1939–40. By war's end, Kaiser had launched an unheard-of 747 ships.

In September 1942, Kaiser invited President Franklin Delano Roosevelt to the launch of the liberty ship SS *Joseph N. Teal* at his Oregon shipbuilding yard. They began fabricating the ship and completed it in just ten days, in time for FDR's visit.

In the spirit of patriotic competition, Kaiser's Richmond

yard vowed to build a liberty ship in only five days. At 12:01 a.m. on Sunday, November 8, 1942, they laid the keel. At 3:27 p.m. on November 12, the SS *Robert E. Peary* launched, four days, fifteen hours, and twenty-six minutes after the keel was laid. This remains the world record for building a ship. This contest inspired the one that takes place in *Poster Girl.*

The term *Wendy the Welder* describes the women who welded and assembled steel plates into troop ships, supply ships, submarines, and aircraft carriers. They played a big role in Kaiser's shipyard. The women welders wore goggles or helmets with dark ultraviolet filtering to protect against *arc eye*, which causes inflammation of the cornea that can burn through to the retina. Many of them suffered first- and second-degree burns. The welding fumes and gases contained heavy metals that created long-lasting health problems. Like the male shipbuilders, they were at risk of a variety of dangers in the shipyard, from electrocution to death by falling.

Wendy the Welder never received the coverage that Rosie the Riveter did, partly because a popular 1943 song, "Rosie the Riveter," and artist Norman Rockwell's famous Rosie *Saturday Evening Post* cover moved her into the popular national consciousness. Perhaps Rosie's most-famous image is the iconic one by artist J. Howard Miller, produced as a work-incentive poster for the Westinghouse Electric & Manufacturing Company. The success of this media coverage was supported by Roosevelt's propaganda group, OWI, the Office of War Information. Many researchers have attempted to discover Rosie's original inspiration. It turns out several women riveters contributed to our vision of the iconic figure.

Though gossip columnist Hedda Hopper initiates the Rosie the Riveter campaign in *Poster Girl*, in real life it happened more organically, with less engineering. Hedda Hopper was not involved.

Inspiration for the novel's character Viviana "Toots" DeNatoli is the most significantly cited real-life Wendy the Welder, Florence "Woo Woo" DiTullio. She was photographed in 1943 by Bernard Hoffman for *Life* magazine. Florence was a twenty-year-old shipyard welder. She wore welding spats, a helmet, with "Flo" painted across the front, and a heavy green welding jacket. It all masked her twenty-year-old figure. Her long auburn braid was the only clue that she was a she. Hiding that was a practical matter in many ways. Florence recalled, "I was a curvaceous one hundred and nineteen pounds. Every time I walked by, the guys would go, 'Woo Woo!'"

As in the novel, a group of female welders did protest in the San Francisco offices of the Boilermakers Union in September of 1942, aiming to be awarded union cards. They were successful, making white women the first union-excluded group to win full admission. By late November 1944, more than three thousand women at Kaiser's Portland shipyard and a similar number in Richmond had received their union cards. The Boilermakers Union now sponsors the Rosie the Riveter World War II Home Front National Historical Park and actively recruits women in the trade.

The US Maritime Commission, in dire need of workers to produce large numbers of ships for the war effort, also required shipbuilding companies to offer jobs to racial minorities who had been excluded from employment. But those opportunities did not equal the jobs offered to white applicants.

Expansion of the shipbuilding industry on the Pacific Coast changed the demography and population dramatically in the East Bay community, Richmond and Oakland in particular. A rapid influx of southern Blacks came to work in the Kaiser and other shipyards. Many came to make better lives for themselves, because Jim Crow laws in the South severely restricted their social and economic mobility.

However, Black workers seeking union membership were blocked by exclusionary union policies, which established separate, auxiliary locals specifically for Blacks. This was common in the Jim Crow South but spread throughout the nation during the war years. The Black auxiliary locals exercised no power, with no union vote or representation at national conventions. The boilermaker auxiliaries were intended to maintain the inferior position of Blacks in this profession.

The memoir of former shipyard employee Betty Reid Soskin, *Sign My Name to Freedom*, is a fascinating account of what it was like for a Black woman to work at those shipyards. She inspired the fictional character Belva Sanders.

Poster Girl's fictional Frank O'Rourke participates in the real-life Doolittle Raid, which took place on April 18, 1942, when the United States bombed Tokyo, and other places on Honshu. The first American air operation to strike the Japanese homeland, the raid caused comparatively minor damage. But it demonstrated that the Japanese mainland was vulnerable to American air attacks. The raid was retaliation for the Japanese attack on Pearl Harbor, providing an important boost to American morale. The raid was planned by, led by, and named after Lieutenant Colonel James "Jimmy" Doolittle.

Sixteen B-25B Mitchell medium bombers, with five-member crews, were launched from the US Navy aircraft carrier USS *Hornet*, in the Pacific Ocean, off Japan, with no fighter escorts. After bombing the military and industrial targets, the crews aimed to land in China.

Of the sixteen crews involved, fourteen returned to the United States or to US forces elsewhere. One crew was killed in action. Eight fliers were captured by Japanese forces in eastern China, and three of these were later executed. All but one of the B-25s were destroyed in crashes, while the sixteenth landed at Vladivostok, in Russia.

Because Russia was not officially at war with Japan, it was required, under international law, to intern the crew during the war, and their B-25 was confiscated. However, within a year, the crew was secretly allowed to leave Russia, pretending to escape. They returned to the United States, or to US units elsewhere, via Allied-occupied Iran and North Africa. Doolittle initially believed that the loss of his aircraft would lead to his court-martial. Instead he received the Medal of Honor and was promoted two ranks to brigadier general. Frank O'Rourke is the fictional pilot of the Vladivostok plane.

Inez Burns is a real-life historical figure, the socialite abortionist of San Francisco. Most details describing her in the novel are taken from her excellent biography by Stephen G. Bloom, *The Audacity of Inez Burns*. Even her cosmetically removed toes and ribs.

Though Jane Benjamin is not based on any single pioneering female journalist, her experiences mirror many of those who fought quiet and not-so-quiet battles to be seen and heard in 1930s and 1940s news pages. She begins to turn herself into someone modeled after Herb Caen, the celebrated six-decade *San Francisco Chronicle* columnist who also came to San Francisco from Sacramento. Caen's "gossip" column was written with humor and thoughtfulness and charm. I hope in this fictional world that Jane can become a journalist in the same vein as Caen. She is certainly trying to do so.

Finally, a word about Sandy Zimmer. Sandy is loosely inspired by Katharine Graham, the stalwart, thirty-year publisher of the *Washington Post*. The first twentieth-century female publisher of a major American newspaper, she presided over the *Post* as it reported on the Watergate scandal, leading to the resignation of President Richard Nixon. Her memoir, *Personal History*, won the Pulitzer Prize in 1998. Sandy's personal details are not at all based on Graham's. But Graham succeeded in a man's world, with savvy, class, guile, and guts. Graham's work and life experience shimmers aspirationally in Sandy's distance.

I'm hoping that Sandy and Jane can continue their partnership well into the twentieth century. But with Jane, you never know. After all, she is a very difficult girl.

I want to send special thanks to the writing and editing people who make my books possible: Brooke Warner, Julie Metz, Shannon Green, Ellen Notbohm, Anne Hawley, Carol Strickland, and my critique group, The RBGs—authors Gretchen Cherington, Ashley E. Sweeney, and Debra Thomas.

I hope you'll join me at www.shelleyblantonstroud.com for further historical details, events, and discussion, as well as information about upcoming novels.

Discussion Questions

1. Mysteries and thrillers are full of "dead girls," often implying that females are especially vulnerable. Why are women the victims in this particular novel? What makes them threatening to the killer?

2. At twenty-two, Jane Benjamin seems cynical about patriotism. Why does she feel this way? Is her cynicism a strength in the circumstance, or a weakness?

3. Most scenes of the novel take place at the Richmond Shipyard, a makeshift city fully created by Lowe Industries. How does this compare to the role of current, large, real-life companies like Amazon and Apple and Facebook, and their effect on the cities where they are built and the people who work there?

4. The women welders in 1942 confront passive resentment and aggressive harassment on the job by some of their male coworkers. Why are some men resentful of the women welders? What are they afraid of? How does this compare to resentment and harassment some women confront in the workplace today?

5. OWI, the Office of War Information, was the propaganda arm of the US war effort, creating not only the iconic posters we still see regularly (*We Can Do It!*) but also radio shows, movies, and magazine articles meant to promote morale and participation in the war economy. Where do you see government and industry propaganda at work today? What is its effect?

6. Over the course of three novels, Jane Benjamin has been aiming for success as a gossip columnist. What does she honestly think about this work? What does she think about the role of truth and lies in the pages of the newspaper? What do you think a journalist must do when telling the truth may endanger people?

7. Hedda Hopper, in particular, is famous for having been a ruthless gossip columnist, especially in her strong support of the House Un-American Activities Committee hearings, for which she named suspected communists and supported the Hollywood blacklist. How does she compare to the media mavens you see today on Twitter and other social media? Are today's Heddas more or less ruthless?

8. Sandy Zimmer does a lot of unpaid, unrecognized work at the *Prospect*. What do you think about her 1940s career path, from secretary to girlfriend to wife to more?

9. Jane is always ambitious and often selfish. What do you think about her trajectory? Can she become a significant columnist by being anything less than that? What do you wish she would do? Would it be possible for her to achieve what she wants if she were less ambitious? Is this different for young women today?

10. What did you think about Inez Burns and her practice as the socialite abortionist of San Francisco? How did the circumstance of her patients compare to that of women seeking abortions today?

11. By the novel's end, it is less than clear what the "right" approach to war might be. What do you think of the conflict between interventionists versus America Firsters in the novel

in 1942, as compared to political conflict in the United States today about the war in Ukraine?

12. What do you think about Jane's possibility of finding love in her life, given her aspirations and her inclinations in 1942? Is it reasonable for a girl like Jane to be hopeful about having the full realm of experience—work and family? Why or why not?

About the Author

Photo credit: Anita Scharf

SHELLEY BLANTON-STROUD grew up in California's Central Valley, the daughter of Dust Bowl immigrants who made good on their ambition to get out of the field. She recently retired from teaching writing at Sacramento State University and still consults with writers in the energy industry. She serves as president of the board of 916 Ink, an arts-based creative writing nonprofit for children, and serves on the board of advisors for the Gould Center for Humanistic Studies at Claremont McKenna College. She previously co-directed Stories on Stage Sacramento, where actors perform the stories of established and emerging authors. She interviews mystery and thriller authors for the Mystery Review Crew. *Copy Boy* is her first Jane Benjamin novel. *Tomboy* is her second. *Poster Girl* is the third. Jane Benjamin has been a finalist in the Sarton Book Awards, IBPA Benjamin Franklin Awards, Killer Nashville Silver Falchion Award, the American Fiction Awards, and the National Indie Excellence Awards. Shelley and her husband live in Sacramento, surrounded by photos of their out-of-town sons, their wonderful partners, their first-ever grandchild, and a lifetime of beloved dogs.

SELECTED TITLES FROM SHE WRITES PRESS

She Writes Press is an independent publishing company founded to serve women writers everywhere. Visit us at www.shewritespress.com.

Copy Boy by Shelley Blanton-Stroud. $16.95, 978-1-63152-697-8. It's 1937. Jane has left her pregnant mother with a man she hates, left her father for dead in an irrigation ditch, remade herself as a man, and gotten a job as a copy boy. And everything's getting better—until her father turns up on her newspaper's front page in a picture that threatens to destroy the life she's making.

Tomboy by Shelley Blanton-Stroud. $17.95. 978-1-64742-407-7. At the peak of Tommie O'Rourke's on-court triumph at the 1939 Wimbledon women's championship, her closest companion, Coach, drops dead of heart attack. Now gossip columnist Jane Benjamin's got to choose: score a big scoop reporting her friend Tommie's private life, or put herself in danger by investigating Coach's murder and its connection to a conspiracy involving US participation in the coming war?

A Child Lost: A Henrietta and Inspector Howard Novel by Michelle Cox. $16.95, 978-1-63152-836-1. Clive and Henrietta are confronted with two cases: a spiritualist woman operating on the edge of town who's been accused of robbing people, and an German immigrant woman who's been lost in the halls of Dunning, the infamous Chicago insane asylum. When a little girl is also mistakenly taken there, the Howards rush to find her, suspecting something darker may be happening . . .

A Girl Like You: A Henrietta and Inspector Howard Novel by Michelle Cox. $16.95, 978-1-63152-016-7. When the floor matron at the dance hall where Henrietta works as a taxi dancer turns up dead, aloof Inspector Clive Howard appears on the scene—and convinces Henrietta to go undercover for him, plunging her into Chicago's gritty underworld.

A Promise Given: A Henrietta and Inspector Howard Novel by Michelle Cox. $16.95, 978-1-63152-373-1. The third installment of the Henrietta and Inspector Howard series unveils the long-awaited wedding of Henrietta and Clive— but murder is never far from this sizzling couple, and when a man is killed on the night of a house party at Clive's ancestral English estate, they are both drawn into the case.